PEGGY GOODY

PEGGY GOODY
DEMODUS

and the

SWORD OF DESTINY

BOOK 2

Charles S. Hudson

Order this book online at www.trafford.com
or email orders@trafford.com

Most Trafford titles are also available at major online book retailers.

Printed in the United States of America.

ISBN: 978-1-4907-1421-9 (sc)
ISBN: 978-1-4907-1422-6 (e)

Trafford rev. 09/11/2013

Trafford
PUBLISHING®   www.trafford.com

North America & international
toll-free: 1 888 232 4444 (USA & Canada)
fax: 812 355 4082

CONTENTS

Chapter 1

SCHOOL HOLIDAYS

P eggy was packing her schoolbooks away and the classroom was buzzing with excitement. It was the last day of term, and the summer holidays were here at last. But Peggy wasn't all that bothered. Ever since Cindy had met Spencer and they had started dating each other, she hardly ever saw her now, apart from school. Peggy had been used to seeing Cindy every day when they were on holiday, but things change in life, and she had to accept it. She had plenty of friends, but no one as close as Cindy had been. They used to go everywhere together.

It made her think about what she might want to do in the future. It was something that she hadn't really thought about until now. She wanted to travel, and visit places that she had read about in her books, and so a career in travel might be the answer. Then she thought of the magic that she possessed, and where that might lead her. She had already worked with the police and the fire department, so they were a possibility.

So much had changed in her life in the last three years, it was sometimes hard to take it all in. The hardest part had been trying to keep the things she did a secret, and act the part of a normal schoolgirl. She had another year at school to think about it, but she did have to give it some serious thought.

When she finished packing her bag, she said goodbye to her friends and her teacher, and started on her way back home. She wasn't in any hurry, and was thinking about what she was going to do to fill her days for six whole weeks. As she got closer to home she could see a long, shiny black car parked in front of the cottage. *Whoever could it be?* she thought. She knew it couldn't be Mr. Flashman, because he had a big Jeep. And as she got up closer to the car, she could see the number plate S M 1. Savajic Menglor; it had to be! She started to run toward the cottage, and now she was feeling really excited. As she got to the door, her heart was thumping. She stopped for a moment and ran her fingers through her hair, then she opened the door. Sitting inside was Savajic Menglor, and next to him was a boy about her own age. He was really handsome, and had thick, black, wavy hair that rested on his broad shoulders.

Savajic jumped to his feet. "Peggy, it's so good to see you again. How are you?"

"I'm very well thank you, Mr. Menglor," replied Peggy. "And how are you?"

"I'm good," he said, and turning to the boy he said, "Peggy, I would like you to meet my son, Owen."

Owen stood up and held out his hand. "I'm very pleased to meet you, Peggy. Father has told me so much about you that I feel I know you already." Peggy held out her hand, and Owen took it and gently shook it.

She was dumbstruck, and all that she could think of to say was, "Hello," but it only took a moment before she was smiling and chatting away.

Rose had made tea and began to pour it. "Do you take sugar, Mr. Menglor?" she asked.

"No thank you," he said, "and please, call me Savajic."

"Very well, and please call me Rose."

They chatted for a while, then Savajic said, "Rose, please let me explain the reason for us visiting you today. I know that this will come as a surprise to you, but first of all, I have to tell you that Owen and I are wizards. Your daughter did me a great service for which I owe her a great debt of gratitude, and hopefully today I have come to repay the debt.

"I would like Peggy to come and stay with us during her summer holiday and learn how to use wizard magic, potions and spells; she will be under my protection at all times, and will come to no harm."

Rose looked bewildered. "You and your son are wizards? But I thought that wizards were in fairy tales!"

Savajic smiled at Rose. "Did you also believe that fairies did not exist, that is, until Peggy showed you her fairy magic?"

"Please excuse me," said Rose, "but all of this is so new to me. I had no idea that Peggy had met you, and even less that she knew that wizards even existed."

"It's a long story, and one that I would relish telling you; but first I need some information from you. Rose, could you tell me if you intend to close the laundry at all during the summer holiday?"

"Well, yes," replied Rose. "We are closing for two weeks, so that we all have our holidays at the same time."

"Excellent!" said Savajic. "Then for those two weeks please say that you will be my guest at my home. I promise that you will have everything that you desire; we have beautiful grounds, a fine boating lake, and a stable, if you like to ride. My chauffer will be at your disposal at all times, should you wish to explore the village."

"You have caught me by surprise," she said, then she took a sip of tea and gave herself a few minutes to think. She put her cup down and said, "I would be delighted to, that is, as long as you are sure it wouldn't put you to any trouble."

"Not at all!" beamed Savajic. "The pleasure will be all mine."

Peggy jumped up and threw her arms around Rose. "Thank you, Mother! I know that you will enjoy yourself, and you deserve a good rest." Then she turned to Savajic and held his hands. She looked directly into his dark-brown eyes, a look that gave him the measure of her affection for him. "Thank you for inviting Mother," she said, and kissed him on the cheek. It was a fleeting moment in time, but greatly appreciated by them both.

"We must make plans," said Savajic. "Rose, will you write down the dates of your two-week holiday and give them to Henry? He will organize the time that he picks you up from home. Now, Peggy, can you be ready to join us in two days' time?"

"Yes!" said Peggy, in an excited voice.

"Then Henry will call you one hour before he starts out," said Savajic. Before they left, Savajic and Owen thanked them again for their hospitality, and said how much they were looking forward to their visit. Then they got into the car and Henry drove off.

Rose sat down at the table and poured herself another cup of tea. "I can't believe all this," she said, looking at Peggy. "Two total strangers turn up on my doorstep, who just happen to be wizards, and within an hour you are going away to learn wizard magic, and I have arranged to have a holiday with a perfect stranger, and I don't even know the destination!"

Peggy was giggling. "I'm so excited!" she said, and put her arms around Rose. "Did you hear what Mr. Menglor said about his house? There is a lake and grounds and horses! It must be lovely, I can't wait!" Rose looked lovingly at Peggy. She was so happy; it was hard to believe how well their fortunes had turned around for the better over the past three years. And she realized how much a part of it was down to Peggy's strong character.

Rose stood up. "Right, young lady, you have two days before you go, so make sure that you have everything ready." Peggy smiled at her, and disappeared upstairs.

THE DREAM

Deep in the forest, Demodus had been very busy since his encounter with Peggy and Bluebell, and the subsequent loss of Savajic's wand. All of his time had been devoted to securing the entrance to his underground kingdom, and he was determined to make sure that there would be no further unwanted visits from Peggy Goody or the fairy world. He had a vast array of intruder alarm technology that he had stolen on his various burglary trips to the human defense factories, and he also had plenty of help from human technicians who were greedy for money.

At the entrance to the caves, a state-of-the-art DNA vibratory ray scanning curtain had been put into place, and could only be passed by someone with Demodom DNA vibrations. The Demodoms would be free to go to the cave where they slept, but nowhere else. The entrance to the laboratory and the firing range would allow entry to Demodus alone, and the same applied to the entrance to his underground mansion. When everything had been tested and proven, Demodus let out a loud sigh of relief. Now the only thing left to do was to take the humans back to where they belonged, and with a very handsome reward for services rendered. They would have no recollection of where they had been, and when they saw the money, Demodus guessed that they wouldn't care.

At last I can relax, he told himself. He was still annoyed with himself for not picking up Peggy Goody's scent; that was, until it was too late to capture her.

That evening after he had finished his dinner, he retired to his study. He sat back in his large, red leather chair and gazed into the air. His mind was fixed on what had happened to Savajic's wand, and how he had been outmaneuvered by a young girl. She seemed to be taking up so much of his time; *why?* he asked himself. He took a gulp of red wine from his tankard; he had lost the chance to capture the powerful fairy Bluebell because Peggy Goody had happened to come along just at the wrong time for the Demodoms, who were lying in wait. But what would make a young girl go wandering alone into the forest? It had to be the fairy's magic that drew her in. And then with another gulp, he drained the last few dregs from the large silver tankard he was drinking from. He was feeling tired and weary, and for the first time in his long life, he felt really old. He gazed up at the ceiling. *Peggy Goody, who are you? What are you?* His heavy eyes slowly closed, and he drifted off into a deep sleep.

Chapter 3

MALAL THE BARBARIAN

A picture appeared in his mind. It was of a beautiful green valley bathed in golden sunlight, and lined with grape vines that stretched as far as the eye could see. In the distance he could see a small village; Gnome women were cooking over a large open fire, and he could see their children. They were running in between the tiny timber houses, laughing and playing games. He could see men working in the fields; they were picking the grapes from the vines and filling their baskets. It was harvest time, and the grapes had already started to be crushed for their rich juice. This was Nectar Valley, the home of the Gnomes' most famous wines. The small village came closer, and he realized that it was the one where he once lived as a small boy.

Then suddenly, without warning, the scene changed violently. He could hear a spine-chilling scream, and from out of nowhere a fearsome band of Barbarians came riding down onto the village. Their horses' hooves pounded the ground like thunder. He could hear the women and children screaming as they dashed for cover into their tiny houses.

The Barbarians were carrying blazing torches, their flames licking wickedly in the air as they rode. They began to set fire to the houses, and as the flames engulfed them, the Gnomes fled from the fire in panic. The Barbarians were waiting for them, and they were charged down and slaughtered one by one. When they were finished, they turned their attention to the men in the vineyard.

The men had heard the screams of their women and were running toward the village; but they were no match. They fought and fought fearlessly, but the Barbarians were showing no mercy. They drove them down through the vines and slaughtered them all. That is, all but one.

Gnomes are natural tunnel diggers, and Jilmin, a young Gnome, had seen the Barbarians coming. He immediately buried himself by boring straight down into the ground, and he didn't stop until he was well out of harm's way.

The Barbarians had not seen him, and he was safe in his underground tunnel. He didn't move for several hours, and then when he thought it was safe to come out, he surfaced again and looked around carefully. He realized that he was all alone. He could see the glow of the Barbarians' fire spitting out sparks into the night sky, and he could hear their drunken laughter. He made quite sure that no one could see him, and then he ran off over the hills to warn the people of Greco, and tell them what had happened to his village. His mission would be to get to Greco and alert King Igor and the Gnome army.

The picture in Demodus' mind went back to the settlement; he could see that the Barbarians were lying around the campfire. Most of them were drunk on the red wine that they had plundered from the vast caves where it was stored. The leader of the Barbarians was Malal, a big, powerful man. He was a vicious killer, and ruled his band of men by fear. He had spared a young girl and had taken her captive. Her name was Mobo, and she was just eighteen years old. He had locked her up in one of the small houses and kept her prisoner for his own amusement.

Jilmin ran and ran, resting only when he was too exhausted to go on, and then only for an hour at the most. As he passed through the small villages on his way to Greco, he alerted the elders to what had happened in Nectar Valley, and warned them to be on their guard. In return, the villagers fed him and gave him a place to rest before he continued on.

It had taken Jilmin two days to get to Greco, and as soon as he had finished telling his story, King Igor called for his army commander, Lettus Beatum. Together they formed a plan of action, and within an hour, fifty soldiers from the Gnome army were mounted on their horses and on their way. They rode their horses hard, and arrived in Nectar Valley at two o'clock the following morning. It was a dark night, but that wasn't going to be a problem for them, because Gnomes can see in the dark.

Thirty soldiers checked their spears and swords, and twenty bowmen checked their arrows; now they were ready to do battle. Commander Beatum gathered his men together. "Listen carefully!" he barked out. "There are twenty-six Barbarians, and fifty of us. This is the plan. They have all been drinking, and seem to be fast asleep. We position ourselves directly over each one of them, and on my signal, thrust your spears into their hearts. We take no prisoners. I repeat, no prisoners. We take nothing for granted. I want the bowmen to circle the camp and be ready to fire your arrows should we have any resistance, and I want the whole thing over within a matter of minutes. We have no need to engage them in a battle, although I do realize that you would all like to hurt them for what they have done to our people. Now let's get to it, and let's make it swift, and clean!"

They moved out silently; the only voice speaking was Beatum's. They had formed a complete circle around the Barbarians and were moving in silently, and as soon as they were in position, Beatum gave the signal. There was no mercy shown; their spears sank deep into the hearts of the Barbarians. That is, all but one. Malal was a warrior with the instincts of a wild animal. He sensed the presence of something standing over him, and as the gnome thrust his spear down toward him, Malal rolled away and was on his feet in a second. His sword flashed in the light of the campfire, and the gnome lay dead. Malal was attacking the gnomes at a frightening speed; five gnomes lay dead before the bowmen managed to down him. It had taken seven arrows buried deep into Malal's chest to stop him, such was his strength. But now he lay there, dead. He was an evil man who had met with a violent death, and now he would never kill again.

As for the rest of the Barbarians, they would never wake from their drunken sleep. It was over and done with before they knew what had hit them. Suddenly a cry rang out, "Commander, we have a survivor!" A soldier had found Mobo. She had been tied up and left on the floor in the house where Malal had kept her his prisoner. Beatum looked at her and he could see how terrified she was. She was sobbing, and couldn't speak. He chose two of his men and told them to get horses and take her back to Greco as soon as possible, and get her cared for.

By dawn the soldiers had built a huge pyre and were placing the bodies of the dead gnomes on top of it. When they had placed the last body in position, they stood back and picked up burning torches. They silently encircled the pyre and stood quietly, with their heads bowed. Lettus Beatum stretched out his arms and looked up at the sky; his loud and long wail could be heard the whole length of the valley. One by one the soldiers threw their burning torches onto the pyre, and the flames rose up into the early morning sky. This was the gnomes' way of releasing their spirits into the sky.

The Barbarians had a very different ending. They were taken out onto the plains, stripped of their clothing, and beheaded. Their bodies were laid out, ready for the vultures to feed on. Their heads were left on the top of spears sticking up from the ground; this was a warning to anyone else that dared attack them ever again.

Chapter 4

DEMODUS THE CHILD

Nine months had passed since the Barbarians' murderous attack had taken place, and Nectar Valley had returned to normal. The small houses had been rebuilt, and new families had settled in. Mobo was being cared for by a childless family; they gave her their friendship and their love. She was about to give birth to Malal's baby, and an elder had been summoned and told that the baby was on its way.

For more than an hour the elder fought to bring the baby out safely. It was enormous, and poor Mobo was so young and so very weak. When at last the baby arrived, it was a boy. He gave out a loud cry, and the elder looked relieved. She picked him up and gave him to Mobo to hold. Mobo cradled him in her arms and kissed him gently; she looked too tiny to have such a large baby. The elder was concerned; she knew that Mobo was not going to survive the birth. Mobo's lips began to move, and the elder leaned in close to her. Mobo's last words were, "Please name my son Demodus, after my father." Then she gave out a long sigh, closed her eyes, and slipped quietly away.

Demodus was still in a deep sleep, but tears were falling from his tired and heavy eyes. He had never known his father or mother, and no one had ever spoken to him about them. He could see the baby being taken away and washed, and then wrapped in a white cloth and laid on a tiny bed. He realized that he was the baby, and watched as the baby grew up. He had many friends to play with, and was a happy child. He could remember so many things.

He had grown into a strong, healthy boy, and was still living with the family who had taken care of his mother. They had been looking after him ever since his mother had died. He already stood out, because even at the age of 10 he was as tall as a fully grown Gnome, and was still growing. His adopted father, Prago, was a kind and generous man who taught him many things. Even at the age of 10 he was able to work by his side in the vineyard. It did not take long before stories of a giant Gnome living in Nectar Valley began to spread across the land.

Chapter 5

VALYEW SELLUM

One day when Demodus was working in the vineyard, a well-dressed stranger approached him. "Good morning!" said the stranger, tipping his hat. "Would you be young Demodus?"

"I am," said Demodus, looking the stranger directly in the eyes. "And who might you be?"

"My name is Valyew Sellum, and I am a prominent merchant from Greco. I have come to ask you if you would like to come and live with me in my home in Greco. Once there you would be schooled, and hopefully gain a good education. I myself would teach you how to buy and sell so that you could learn to trade and become a merchant like myself. You would also be expected to spend a period of time with the army, where you would learn how to fight and how to defend yourself. And then when you are fully trained, you will be ready to join me on my many trips to far-off lands. You will become my companion and my bodyguard, and protect me. So, Demodus, how does all of that sound to you?"

Demodus was still young, but even at his age he was not looking forward to spending the rest of his life growing grapes. He had his father's urge to be free and travel the world. Demodus looked Valyew in the eyes with a defiant stare; Valyew's eyes didn't even flicker. For a long two minutes their eyes were locked, probing each other's thoughts, then suddenly, without any reservation, Demodus declared, "Yes, I would like to come and live with you very much. But you do know that you would have to get permission from my parents."

"That shouldn't be too much of a problem," said Valyew. "I am a very wealthy man, and can compensate them greatly for their loss."

Valyew did the deal, and Demodus said goodbye to his adopted parents. It wasn't all that hard for him, though. They had looked after him very well, but there was not the love bond of a real mother and father.

And so it was that Demodus left his home in Nectar Valley and went to live with Valyew Sellum in Greco.

Chapter 6

A NEW BEGINNING

Valyew gave Demodus his first horse. "This is for you," he said. "And please, try not to fall off it too many times." Demodus mounted the horse and never looked like he would be falling off, because like his father, he was a natural-born rider.

When they arrived at the home of Valyew Sellum, Demodus was amazed. It was a magnificent white palace surrounded by beautiful gardens and trees, and as they passed through a wonderfully carved archway, they came into another garden inside, with a massive pool in the center. Valyew was carefully watching Demodus' reaction. "I can see that you like my home, Demodus," he said. "Although, I do have to admit that the design is not all mine. I got the idea for it when I was on my travels. I was trading in a city called Rome at the time; a smelly place, but quite beautiful. Some very clever people live there, and they have plenty of gold. Perhaps I will take you with me in the future when I am trading there." (If Valyew could have seen into the future, he would never have made such a promise to take Demodus there.)

When they went inside, Demodus could see just how wealthy Valyew was. Room after room was filled with fine furniture and ornate figures of silver and gold. "Do you like what you see, Demodus?" he asked. "Because it came at great cost and many years of hard work."

"I want you to remember this, Demodus and never ever forget it; gold is king. Gold will get you anything that you desire, and gold will never let you down."

"I won't forget," said Demodus, looking puzzled, and not really knowing what Valyew Sellum meant.

The first thing that Demodus learned was just how good a hot bath felt, and he loved having scented oils rubbed onto his body and hair by one of the many female servants that Sellum had. Then he learned how good it felt to wear fine clothes, and how soft they felt next to his skin. Valyew came in to see how he was doing. "That's much better," he said. "You clean up quite well. Tonight, Demodus, you will find out the delights of eating at the house of Valyew Sellum."

Demodus was seated next to Valyew in the great central room, and in front of them was a feast to behold. Valyew clapped his hands and gave the command, "Begin."

Music began to float into the room, and six dancing girls poured out into the room from one side. They started to perform their dance, much to the delight of Valyew. He turned to Demodus. "Eat, boy, eat." Demodus was beginning to understand what Valyew had meant when he was talking about gold. This was the life of a king, and you could live it if you had enough gold. Demodus was still very young, but he made his mind up there and then that someday he would possess as much gold as Valyew, perhaps even more.

Chapter 7

DEMODUS THE MAN

Ten more years passed, and now Demodus was fully grown. He was a hand short of six feet six inches tall, a giant Gnome with a powerful, sculptured physique. He had learned his lessons well, and with Valyew's encouragement, he was becoming a very wealthy merchant. He was the pride and joy of Valyew, and in return, Demodus was devoted to him, and protected him from any danger that came to pass on their many journeys around the world. Demodus was also a fearsome warrior, and had fought many battles in strange lands for gold. He had never even come close to being beaten.

Valyew had taken him to Rome and presented him to the Emperor. "Fight for me in the coliseum," pleaded the emperor. Demodus fought there for thirty days. He conquered everything that was pitted against him, from small groups of gladiators, to chariots with bowmen. He even fought a wild bull and a brown bear, and he was fearless and unstoppable.

The Emperor lavished Demodus with the highest honors of Rome, and much gold. The Emperor begged Valyew to sell Demodus to him, to which Valyew replied, "Demodus is not a slave, he is my son, and no amount of gold could ever replace him." The Emperor reluctantly accepted Valyew's answer, but made him promise to return to Rome in the future.

The emperor was not an honorable man; he didn't need to be, because he thought he was a god. Even before Valyew and Demodus had started their journey back home, the Emperor was plotting to kill Valyew and have Demodus brought back as a slave. Then he would make him fight as a gladiator for his own entertainment.

He had called for his personal guard and made plans for him to enlist twenty of his finest men. They were to make sure that Valyew and his caravan were well away from the city, and attack them when they entered the pass that ran through the gorge. Their orders were to kill everyone except for Demodus; he was to be taken prisoner and returned to the coliseum and locked away. The soldiers' payment would be all of the gold that the caravan carried. The Emperor said to them that when they had Demodus safely locked away, they could share it all among themselves.

Valyew and Demodus had a caravan of some thirty wagons, and as they moved through the city gates, the crowds were shouting and calling out to Demodus; he was very much their champion. The caravan moved at a steady pace, and four hours later it was approaching the gorge. The soldiers had ridden out before the caravan had left the city and were waiting hidden in the rocks, ready for the signal to attack. What they did not know was that Demodus had a strategy he used whenever the caravan had to pass through high rocks. He would go ahead on his own and climb up and check to make sure that there were no thieves hiding and waiting to rob them.

He could not believe his eyes when he spotted the soldiers. Not thinking that he was in any kind of danger, he walked straight toward them. "Demodus!" one soldier shouted. "It's Demodus; quick, don't let him escape!" Those were the last words that he would ever say. Demodus realized in a flash what was happening; rogue soldiers trying to rob them of their gold. He tore into them with a frightening ferocity; he spun and twisted his claws, slashing through the soldiers' uniforms as if they were made of paper. For twenty minutes Demodus battled with the soldiers. They were all very well-trained, and he had to be aware that he was in terrible danger. At last it was over. The soldiers all lay dead, scattered among the rocks, and he sank to the ground, wounded and exhausted.

When the caravan reached the entrance to the gorge it stopped, and Valyew shouted out, "Demodus, where are you?" Just as he did, Demodus came staggering toward him. As he got up close, Valyew could see that he was covered in blood. Demodus called out for water, and collapsed. After he had gulped down a ladle of water, he began to mumble to Valyew what had happened, and then passed out. They would never know that the soldiers were there by order of the Emperor; but there and then they decided that they would never go back to Rome.

It was the first time that Valyew had seen Demodus really wounded. He'd had the odd cuts and bruises before, but this time he had almost met his match, and could have paid dearly.

The caravan pulled away slowly, with Demodus lying on his back, having his wounds tended. It would take two days before he sat up and spoke to Valyew.

In Rome, another scenario was playing out. One of the soldiers had fled the battle, terrified that Demodus would kill him. He stood before the Emperor, trembling, and gave his story to him. He told how Demodus had surprised them as they lay in wait among the rocks. They had netted him, but he had ripped the nets to shreds with his razor-sharp claws and was killing them off, one by one. Then he told the Emperor that he had plunged his spear into Demodus' heart, killing him. He said that he was the last soldier standing, and he had no choice. The Emperor shrugged his shoulders and said, "Well, at least if I can't have him, neither can anyone else. There is no need to pursue the caravan; let them go on their way."

The only concern that Valyew had ever had about Demodus was his thirst for fighting and killing, although there had never, ever been a cross word between the two of them. But he was terrified that someday Demodus would meet his match and be killed, and then he would lose the only thing in the world that he had ever loved more than gold. Today was proof that sometime in the future, Demodus might be set upon and overwhelmed by numbers.

He had spoken to Demodus at length about the dangers of fighting for gold, but Demodus would pick him up and spin him around, laughing out loud. "It's only for a bit of fun when I'm bored on a long trip. I do not want you to worry about me, Valyew. I have never met a creature yet that can stand against my sword and my claws."

Valyew had looked at him and said, "Demodus, when I die, everything that I possess will be yours. I just want you to be here to enjoy it all."

"I will be," said Demodus. Then he suddenly looked seriously at Valyew. "You are not ill, are you?"

"No," said Valyew, "but I'm not getting any younger, either. And although we are not of the same blood, you are the son that I had always dreamed of, and the only son that I would ever want."

Demodus put his powerful arms around Valyew and said, "And you are the finest father a man could ever wish for."

Valyew said, "Demodus, my son, there is something that I want you to have." He pulled at a gold chain that hung around his neck. On the end of it was a large tiger's tooth.

Demodus looked at it; it was large and curved, and on the top was a gold cap. "What is it?" he asked Valyew.

Chapter 8

THE EYE OF GLINT

Valyew held the tiger's tooth in his hand and looked down at it and said, "It goes back a very long time; in fact, some three hundred years. I was travelling through the valley of the Fladonion people about five hundred miles north of the Great Black Desert. They were a race of kind and simple people that lived off the land, and they worshiped their all-seeing god, Glint. But for the previous four years their crops had failed, and they were hungry and had lost faith in their god.

"When I arrived at the city gates I could see a large crowd of people demonstrating in the city square, demanding grain from the stock that was put aside for planting the following year's crop. They were obviously very hungry and looking to feed their children.

"I happened to be carrying one hundred and eighty sacks of grain in four of my wagons, and made a very unusual trade. The statue of their god Glint had a large crystal eye in the center of his head, and it was claimed that even a blind man could gaze into it and see all. The people were on the verge of starving, and after much bargaining, I managed to make a trade with their leader. I would give them all of my grain in exchange for the eye of Glint. The Fladonion people believed that Glint had brought me to them to save them from starving, and gave up the eye willingly.

"For many years on my travels I had amused myself by looking into it and seeing many wonderful things; it was a good companion.

"One day on a trip up into the Mountains of the Blue Moon, I happened to hear a story of an old man who claimed to be a wizard, and was over one thousand years old. It was said that he lived in a cave high in the mountains, and was a magic man. He had been blind for fifty years, and said that he was the oldest wizard alive.

"When he was a young boy he claimed to have been taught his lessons at a place called the Black Eagle School for Wizards, in a far-off land. When he was a young wizard, he had devoted himself to the mysteries of alchemy. He had studied for many years, and discovered many powerful and potent potions.

"He had left home and travelled the world in search of rare elements and exotic plants, and eventually he had found the secret compound for everlasting life. As we talked, I realized that he really was very old. He spoke of his entire family being killed in a wizard war long ago. He feared that if he returned home, he would become a target, and then the greatest find of all time, Eternal Life, may fall into the wrong hands.

"Around his neck was a tiger tooth on a gold chain, the very same one that I wear today. He claimed that inside it was the magic compound that would give eternal life to whoever wore it. And it was impossible to steal, because it could only be removed by the person wearing it.

"Then he made an unbelievable statement; he said that he was tired of being blind and old, and would trade the tooth with anyone that could make him see again. Then he would be able to live the last years of his life gazing down once more at the world below.

"It was an opportunity not to be missed. I produced the eye of Glint and asked the old wizard to gaze into it, and his response was overwhelming. 'I can see, I can see!' he cried. One hour later I was walking out of his cave wearing the tiger tooth; that was two hundred and sixty years ago.

"I thought it was the most valuable treasure that I possessed, even greater than my gold. But over the past years I have come to realize that it isn't; you are, my son. And because of this, I want you to wear it for me, and always remember me when you look at it."

Demodus stood up; he towered over Valyew. "Do you really think that I would strip you of your protection? I am still young and strong. And why do you think that I would come to any harm? I wear my dragon-skin robe when I fight, and nothing can pierce it. If a dragon cannot stand against me, then who can?"

"But it doesn't cover all of you," protested Valyew, "and you only wear it when you take on a challenge. Have you learned nothing from our trip to Rome? It would make me very proud and happy if you wore it for me, and I still have you to look after me."

Demodus knelt down, and Valyew passed on to him his great treasure.

THE PYTHON

Over the next ten years, Valyew and Demodus travelled the world, trading their various cargos. They had seen many wonderful and magical things. They had both watched a boy sit on a magic carpet and rise into the air and fly around in the sky.

In another land they had seen a man in the marketplace play on a flute, and a rope had risen from out of a basket and into the sky. Then a young boy had climbed the rope and disappeared, and the rope had fallen back down into the basket.

They had met many magic men on their travels. One day they came across a snake charmer playing his flute in the market place, and they stopped to watch. The snake was a python, with long fangs. It swayed to the rhythm of the music, and although it was deadly, it looked quite beautiful.

Then suddenly, without warning, three horsemen came galloping through the market. One of them hit Valyew and knocked him onto the snake. Before anyone could react, the python had sunk its fangs deep into Valyew's neck. Demodus had jumped in and grabbed the python and ripped it to pieces in seconds, but it was too late. The venom was already coursing through Valyew's veins. Two minutes later, he was dead. The scream that Demodus let out sent everyone running for their lives. In his rage, he smashed everything in sight. Then as his rage calmed, he cradled Valyew in his arms and wept. If only Valyew had been wearing the tiger tooth around his neck, he would have still been alive. He thought about ripping it off and throwing it as far away as he could. Then he remembered Valyew's words, "Wear it with pride and when you touch it, think of me."

An hour later, Demodus had buried Valyew. Then he tethered all the horses at a stable next to the market. He mounted his own horse and galloped off in pursuit of the three riders that had caused Valyew's death. He hunted them down like a hungry tiger; he crossed the plain and two rivers, and caught up with them at the edge of a forest. It was early morning, and Demodus could see the smoke rising from their campfire. He rode in, dismounted, and told them what they had done.

Then they made the terrible mistake of laughing at him. Within fifteen minutes they were hanging from the branches of a large tree. Demodus had stripped off their clothes and was talking to them in a menacing voice. "So, tell me before you die; which one of you still thinks that causing my father's death is funny?" The three riders were now sobbing and begging for mercy. Their pleas were met by a stony wall of silence. Slowly Demodus lifted his hand, and his claws came out. Then one by one, he ripped them open.

As he rode away, the screams faded into the distance. He was crying uncontrollably. Looking up to the sky he screamed, "Forgive me, Father, you trusted me, and I let you down."

For three years he wandered around the world, drinking and fighting until he was exhausted and had no fight left in him. Then he went home. Demodus would never travel and trade again.

Chapter 10

GRIEF AND GOLD

Demodus had all the wealth that he could ever want, and yet it all seemed to be pointless without Valyew at his side. He had no desire to travel around the world trading, or even fighting for gold, which was once such a passion of his. He was changing, and there was nothing that he could do to stop it from happening; Valyew was on his mind constantly. Demodus was a regular visitor at the palace and a favorite of the king, but even that and all the fame he had for being the king's champion was somehow not enough.

Then one day, everything seemed to become clear. He could remember Valyew speaking to him when he first came to live with him. His words filled his head. *Gold is king; gold will get you anything that you desire; gold will never let you down.*

Demodus had his thoughts twisted and distorted with grief, but now he had a mission; he would own more gold than anyone else in the land. But how? He lay back on a pile of soft cushions and closed his eyes. Who would have more gold than he? He'd amassed his own gold, and now with Valyew's gold added, it was a vast amount. He kept his gold in the Rainbow Bank. But who had more?

Then a thought came into his head; *the Rainbow Bank has it all.* If he could somehow tunnel under the bank and come up into the vaults, he could transfer gold from other vaults into his own, and no one would ever know. It was a master plan that couldn't possibly go wrong.

Two days later, Demodus had pitched a camp in the trees five hundred yards from the back of the Rainbow Bank. It would require a lot of tunneling, but once there, he would be able to take his time. He began to tunnel his way toward the bank, and it took several hours. But at last he made it. He was standing at the bottom of a massive cave. As he looked up, he could see how the rock had been mined out to form a slow spiral running down from the bank, so that the Leprechauns could walk up and down, transferring gold to the various vaults. The spiral ended some twenty yards above him, but he would have no trouble climbing up to it. He had a second key to his own vault and knew exactly where it was, but he had to capture the Leprechaun guard, and get hold of his keys. He had come prepared; he brought a rope, a gag, and a blindfold, and his plan was to capture the Leprechaun that was on guard, and then gag him, blindfold him and tie him to his chair.

Demodus had estimated that a maximum of five vaults would be his target. He knew that he would have to move the gold from the five vaults and into his own as quickly as possible, and then he would release the Leprechaun. Hopefully by the time he had taken off the blindfold and the gag, Demodus would have climbed back down to the bottom of the cave and disappeared down into his tunnel, covering his tracks behind him.

He stood motionless in the dark; he knew that there would be no second chance. From the moment he captured the guard, he would have to move quickly. The slightest hesitation could ruin the whole plan. He decided that the best plan was to rob the five vaults leading up to his vault, and that would keep the distance between the vaults to a minimum, and give him more time to carry the gold.

He watched carefully as the guard approached the bottom of the spiral. He sat down and rested for a few minutes, and then started to walk back up the spiral.

Demodus began to count; he could hear the *tap, tap* of the Leprechaun's stick as he walked back up the spiral pathway, and that came as a sharp reminder to him of the magic power that the Leprechaun's stick possessed. He would have to be very careful not to give him time to point it at him. He had counted up to nine hundred when he heard the guard stop and talk to someone; it must be another guard standing at the back entrance to the bank. He calculated that he would have about fifteen minutes to complete the whole operation; two minutes for each vault, and five minutes to capture and bind the guard, and then release him after the robbery and make his getaway.

He took a deep breath and began to climb; he positioned himself just out of sight at the bottom of the spiral path, and then got ready to pounce on the guard as soon as he sat down and turned his back to him. The guard seemed to take forever coming back; the seconds felt like minutes to him. Then suddenly he was there next to him, and as he turned and sat down, Demodus leapt. He overpowered him and bound his hands behind his back in seconds. Then he took the guard's stick and threw it down onto the floor of the cave; he wasn't taking any chances. Within seconds he was opening the first vault; inside was a treasure. He picked up five heavy ingots of gold, stepped outside and locked the heavy door. He put them down outside his own vault and went back for more. He took five ingots from each vault, then he placed them down carefully into his own vault, and locked the door behind him and ran back down to the guard. He had only taken ten minutes for the whole operation. He took his time and untied the rope that was binding the guard's hands. "Don't move," he hissed, and then he climbed back down to the floor of the cave and made his escape.

As he surfaced, the rush of fresh air felt good on his face. He was feeling very happy with himself; *the perfect robbery,* he said to himself. *The bank has been robbed, but the bank still has the gold!* He gave out a wicked laugh, then he set about cleaning up the campsite, removing all traces of him ever being there, and then he went home.

Chapter 11

PANIC AT THE BANK

I n the Rainbow Bank there was panic; had there been a robbery? If so, what had been stolen? There were no traces of a robbery. There were no traces of anything except for the rope, the gag, and the blindfold, and they could have come from anywhere.

Elkin, the head of the bank, was questioning the poor unfortunate guard. "You must have seen something. Someone doesn't just come out of thin air and tie you up. You must have at least *heard* something."

"It was how I told you the first time, Elkin. I didn't hear or see anything!" Then he stopped. "Wait! I did hear something; I heard vault doors opening and closing."

"Excellent!" said Elkin. "Now we know that it's possible that some of the vaults could have been robbed. Now then, try and think back to when you heard the doors open and close. How far away from you do you think it was?"

The guard closed his eyes and concentrated. Then after a few minutes he said, "At least halfway up the spiral, maybe more."

"That's good enough," said Elkin. "You may have just saved the day!"

Elkin was back in the bank, giving out orders. He had picked four of his most experienced men. "We start at vault number three hundred and seventy-eight, and work our way up four vaults at a time. Look for high-value pieces, and as soon as you find that something is missing, summon me immediately. Is that clear?"

"Yes, Elkin," they replied.

"Well then, let's get going."

Two hours later a voice shouted, "I've found something!"

Elkin was called. "What have you found?" he asked.

One of his men was pointing to his register. "There are five bars of gold missing from this vault."

"Good work," said Elkin. "Now let us open up the next four vaults, and see what we find." The next four vaults were opened and found to be five bars of gold short in each. "And now another four vaults, if you please," said Elkin.

"Here!" shouted one of the men; it was the very next vault. When he swung the door open, there were gasps of disbelief. Lying neatly stacked on the floor were twenty-five gold bars, and according to the register, that was twenty-five too many.

"Bring your register to my room," said Elkin, and turning to the others he gave a stern order: "This goes no further. Do I make myself clear?"

"Yes, Elkin," they all answered.

Back up in his room, Elkin looked at the name on the register; it was the Gnome Demodus, the merchant and famous warrior. He stroked his beard thoughtfully and said, "I can't understand this. Demodus is already one of the richest Gnomes in Greco. Why would he need to steal from others? We need to think this one out. Let us remember that Demodus has killed many times and in many different lands; he must have made enemies along the way. What if *he* isn't the thief, but someone else would want us to *think* that he was? We have to be very careful what we do. In the meantime, let us make sure that the gold bars are returned to the rightful owners, and in the next few days, we will have to come up with a plan."

The next day Elkin got in contact with the Golden Fairy Queen; she had helped the Leprechauns set up the Rainbow Bank in the beginning, and had put large deposits of gold in the very first vault to get them going. Elkin explained what had happened at the bank the day before and who the main suspect was, but the problem was that Demodus was already one of the richest gnomes, so he would have no motive.

"Greed is a powerful motive," replied the Queen, "so do not rule him out, because if it is greed on his behalf, he will surely try again.

"You tell me that the gold has been returned to the rightful owners, so should he not try again, then nothing will be lost. But my instinct tells me that if nothing is said about a robbery at the bank, he will think that he has got away with it, and it is almost certain that he will try again.

"From today I will scan an area within a radius of one mile from the bank, and if he comes into the area, I will see him. I will tell you of his presence, and you can set up a trap. Let him into the bank unhindered, and let him capture the guard again. You must let him actually start to steal from the vaults;

only then can you attack him. Chase him up the spiral and through the bank into the open, and then I will do the rest. And, Elkin, please make sure that your guards have plenty of power in their sticks."

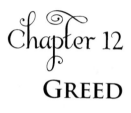

Chapter 12

GREED

Demodus had waited patiently for five weeks, expecting to hear news of a robbery at the Rainbow Bank, but there was nothing, no news at all. He let out a crazy-sounding laugh. The guard must have been so afraid that he had hidden the rope and the gag and the blindfold by throwing them down onto the floor of the cave, and hoped that no one would ever find out what had happened.

It had all been so simple, so very easy, and he had gotten away with it. Clouded by his own conceit, he decided it was time to rob the bank again. Why not? No harm had been done after all, and the bank had plenty of gold. He paced around the room, mumbling to himself. "Yes," he said out loud; it was time to strike again. Tomorrow he would make preparations, but for now, he would sleep.

Morning came, and Demodus was awake and ready for his task. He would set up his camp today and keep watch, and then tomorrow he would rob the bank once again. He was so excited; it was all so easy, he almost felt sorry for the bank.

Later in the day, the Golden Fairy Queen had a clear picture of Demodus in the pool of wisdom. She watched as he set up his camp and then spied on the bank, and when the bank closed, he went home. The Queen watched him until he disappeared from her view.

The Queen had contacted Elkin earlier in the day and told him to be prepared, for she was certain that Demodus was getting ready to strike the next day. Elkin said that he would have everyone in place and out of sight. The plan was to let Demodus enter the cave and climb up to the bottom of the spiral path, and capture and tie up the guard. Then he would be allowed to reach the vault that he intended to rob, and open the door. Once Demodus was inside the vault, three guards that would be hiding in the bottom vault would jump out and chase him up the slope toward the bank. He was to be allowed to run though the bank unhindered, and when he got outside, he would be at the mercy of the Golden Fairy Queen, who would deal with him in her own way.

Chapter 13

THE TRAP

E arly next morning, Demodus was preparing himself for the raid on the bank. He was surprised by how relaxed he felt; but he told himself that he must never let his guard down, not even for a moment. All the things that he needed were already at his campsite, so he started out at a brisk pace. As soon as he arrived at his camp, he gathered the things that he would need, and began to tunnel toward the cave directly under the bank. As he broke through the rubble that lay at the bottom of the cave, he was hit by the silence; he hadn't noticed it before. He shook his head and started to climb up to the spiral path, and as he reached it, he froze; the guard was already there, and was just about to turn around and walk back up the spiral path. He pounced and had the guard bound, gagged, and blindfolded in seconds, and was on his way up to the vaults. His plan was different this time; he had decided to rob the five vaults *after* his vault, instead of the five vaults in front, like he had done last time.

This was the last thing the Leprechauns needed; a change of plan. It meant that when they came out of the bottom vault where they were hiding, Demodus would be facing them, and he would have the advantage of seeing the vault door open before they were even out of the vault.

Demodus reached his own vault and unlocked the door, then he moved up to the next vault. He put the key in the door and turned it; in the same moment that he turned the key, his eyes caught a movement below him. His head turned as the door to the bottom vault opened; he saw a stick come out, and he knew it was a trap. His warrior instinct kicked in, and he was already running at full speed toward the bottom of the spiral path. His claws were out, and it was a frightening sight; the Leprechaun guards didn't even have a chance to raise their sticks. They were still coming out of the vault, and totally unaware of what was on its way to meet them. It was as though the trap had been reversed. Demodus smashed into them with such ferocity that they were dead in seconds, ripped to shreds by his razor-sharp claws. He didn't stop to look back. He ran past the guard that he had bound up, and jumped off the end of the spiral path. His body twisted in the air and started to spin. He hit the bottom of the cave claws-first and disappeared into the ground before the guards above even knew what was happening.

Demodus came back up into the sunlight and fresh air. His head was spinning. *How did they know that I would be there?* he asked himself. He had underestimated the guard from the first robbery. He must have admitted to being captured, but he hadn't seen who it was, so the trap could have been set for anyone. The three guards that were there to trap him were all dead, and the other guard was blindfolded, so no one would ever know that it was him. He sat for a while, letting the events of the past hour sink in. It was unfortunate that he had killed the three Leprechauns. He didn't want it, but they might have killed him; it was self-defense, he told himself. He was a killer by nature, and now he was also a murderer and a thief. The events of the last hour suddenly hit him, and a deep sense of remorse came over him. He had not felt such pain since Valyew Sellum had died. Tears began to run down his face, and he sobbed uncontrollably. He sat there, wondering how could he have been so stupid and so greedy, and how could he ever hold his head up high again?

Back at the Rainbow Bank there was total panic. Within minutes after Demodus had escaped, the alarm had been raised, and then the terrible realization of what had happened became apparent. Elkin had dashed from the bank to tell the Golden Fairy Queen what had happened and as soon as he was finished, she transported to the camp of Demodus. She waited and watched as he appeared from out of the ground. He was covered in blood, and he was panting heavily. She let him wash and change his clothes, and she watched as he sat down. It seemed that he was talking to himself. She watched as he put his head in his hands and began to weep. After a short rest he got up, wiped his face, and began to pack a large bag, which he tied at the top and threw over his shoulder. He had a grim look on his face as he started to walk away; that was when he came to a stop and couldn't move. "Your freedom is over, Demodus," said the Queen, and disappeared.

After the Queen had informed Elkin that Demodus had been captured, she told him that he would be handed over to King Igor in Greco to be put on trial and punished for robbery and murder, under Gnome Law.

Chapter 14
THE TRIAL

In his dream state, Demodus could see the scene of his trial in Greco. For robbing the Rainbow Bank and the murder of three Leprechauns, he faced a possible sentence of death. He saw himself standing in the great hall of the palace, his head bowed before Igor, his King, and the Elders.

Many high-ranking gnomes spoke up for him. They told of all the honors that he had gained for the gnome kingdom. They told of all the things that he had done for the old and poor gnomes. One by one they pleaded for Demodus to be spared from the death sentence. Igor stood up and addressed the great hall. "Today is the saddest day of my life. Not only is Demodus our greatest champion, he is also a personal friend, and a friend of the whole Gnome nation. I know that when his father Valyew Sellum died it had a devastating effect on Demodus, and I can only believe that this has led to this madness that has taken him over."

"Nevertheless, nothing excuses robbery and murder. You have brought disgrace to the Gnome World, and to the name of Valyew Sellum, and for your evil actions you will be banished to the wilderness of the Arctic, where you will live out your life with the polar bears and the seals. The power to see in the dark and your ability to tunnel and your gnome sense of direction will be your only means of surviving. You have been the Gnomes' most famous warrior, so you have all the tools to survive. That is my sentence. Goodbye, my friend and good luck." The King turned and walked away. His head was bowed, and he was crying. He didn't look up until he was out of sight.

As Demodus left the palace, a massive crowd had assembled outside. The sentence had filtered out to them and they were calling out Demodus: "We will never forget you! You will always be in our hearts and our thoughts!"

It was decided that the house of Demodus would be kept and opened up as a museum, with all his trophies and weapons on display. The stone statue of him that stood in the city square would be moved and put onto the grounds of his house. There would also be a large plaque put up telling of his madness on the day that he robbed the Rainbow Bank.

Chapter 15

THE JOURNEY

For five hundred years he wandered the icy wastes of the Arctic, honing his hunting skills, catching fish and seals to survive. And all the time his body had been changing to adapt to the freezing-cold snow storms and the ice-cold water. His feet had grown wider and his toes were webbed, allowing him to walk on the surface of the snow. His body grew a thick layer of fine, reddish-colored hair that kept out the harsh Arctic wind and stopped him from freezing. His head had changed most of all; it was fish-like. His large ears had almost disappeared, leaving tiny holes. He had bulging eyes with heavy lids and a flat nose, and his mouth was large and wide, with thick, protruding lips.

His hunting skills were awesome. His ability to tunnel at high speed through the ice and come up directly underneath his prey gave them no chance to escape his slashing, vicious claws. He had also grown in stature; he was bear-like, with big shoulders and strong, muscular arms. His legs were thick and powerful from years of walking against the strong winds on the ice plains. His height had increased to a staggering six-foot-six plus. He was king of this harsh and barren wilderness, and even the mighty polar bear kept a safe distance between him and themselves ever since he had killed one of them.

It had happened on a freezing-cold day in the middle of winter. He had just emerged from his underground cave when he heard an ear-shattering roar. It was a massive female polar bear. Before he had time to react, she had knocked him off his feet, and fortunately for him, sent him spinning away from her. He got up and saw her coming toward him. His claws came out, and he was spinning down into the ice before she could get to him. He had never been attacked by a polar bear before, but now it was her or him. He kept on tunneling until he was directly underneath her, then he took a deep breath and pushed up, spinning as fast as he could. As he broke through the surface of the ice she had no chance of moving, and her legs were cut to pieces. Demodus stood over her and watched her die, and as he looked at her he thought, *What a terrible waste of a life; she was such a beautiful creature.*

Then from behind a snow drift he could hear a soft cry. He walked over to where the noise came from and to his surprise, there were two small baby bears. He moved over to them and realized that they were hungry and that their mother had been looking for food for them. He knew that if he left them there they would die, so he picked them up and took them back to his cave. For the next two years he fed them and looked after them, keeping them safe in his cave.

Demodus and the bears lived happily together as a family for some fifty years. They would roam the ice plains together, hunting. Now that the bears were fully grown, they towered over Demodus. No creature would ever dare challenge them. But the bears grew old, and one night they both lay down and went to sleep, never to wake again. Demodus was broken-hearted and alone again, and he knew that as long as he wore the tiger tooth, he would be there forever.

It was sheer loneliness that eventually drove him to move south. The Gnome world would surely have forgotten about him by now, and most of the Gnome people that he knew would have died long ago. And now, surely no one would think that he was still alive and try to stop him. He was right, and he began his journey south unhindered.

He took his time travelling, taking in all the wonderful new sights, staying in some places longer than others. He took great pleasure in riding on the massive ice flows that drifted south. Then one day he drifted into what he thought was the most beautiful place that he had ever seen. He was in the fjords, narrow inlets of sea in between high cliffs. Without knowing it, he had reached a new land.

When he looked around, he decided that it would be a good place to live for a time, and so he dove off the ice that had brought him there and swam over to the rocks. He climbed up the rock face until he found a large ledge jutting out, and he began to tunnel deep into the rock. After about twenty yards, the rock in front of him suddenly gave way and revealed a massive cave. He scrambled inside, and in the middle of the cave was a bright, golden glow that lit up the whole cave. He slowly moved toward it, and as he got up close to the light source, he could see that it was a sword. It had a jet-black hilt with a dark-red hand grip and what looked like flames running up the bottom part of the blade. The blade shone like a mirror, and inscribed on it were the words: SWORD OF DESTINY. Written in the rock that held the sword were the words: HE WHO DRAWS AND WIELDS THIS SWORD IN BATTLE WILL BE MASTER OF HIS OWN DESTINY. Demodus just looked at it and shrugged his shoulders. "Who cares?" he mumbled to himself. But as he looked around, he thought the cave would be perfect for his new home, and it was going to save him a lot of hard work.

His time in the Arctic had made him a wonderful underwater swimmer, and he had perfected a style that closely resembled that of a seal. It was strong and fast, and he could stay underwater for up to twenty minutes. It had been a perfect preparation for his new home. As he became accustomed to his new surroundings, his life suddenly became enjoyable again. He had more than enough to eat, and the weather was much warmer. He was once again conscious of the changing seasons.

It was on one of the long summer nights as he sat at the entrance to his cave, watching the birds as they swooped down onto the fjord catching the small fish that came up to the surface to eat the insects that hovered above the water, when something else caught his eye. He noticed a movement on the rocks below. He lay motionless as he stared down onto the rocks by the water's edge; he was about to encounter the Scaleygills.

Chapter 16

THE SCALEYGILLS

He moved down the side of the cliff and slid slowly into the water without even making a ripple. He was in hunting mode, and he took a deep breath and sank down beneath the surface of the water. He could see quite clearly underwater, because in his many years swimming in the Arctic waters, he had developed a second transparent eyelid that automatically closed when he went underwater. And as he watched, he was fascinated by what he saw. There must have been hundreds of them; creatures that looked like large lizards, but instead of four legs, they had arms and hands and stood upright on their legs, and their heads were strangely human-like.

Demodus dove down deeper and deeper, and all he could see were the creatures. Then he realized that they had seen him, too. They were circling around him and closing in above, in an attempt to weigh him down and drown him. He forced his powerful arms up above his head and opened his razor-sharp claws to tunneling position. Then he spun his body and kicked up toward the surface. It was sheer carnage; his claws sliced through their bodies like butter. There was no time for them to move out of his way, such was his speed and power. He hit the surface with so much force that the creatures scattered in all directions in a desperate race to escape from him.

He pulled himself up onto the rocks and looked around. The fjord was a reddish color, and it had creatures floating all around in it. He had not wanted to harm them, he told himself, but they had tried to kill him. What else could he have done? He sat there thinking about what had just taken place, and he watched as the bodies of the creatures slowly sank into the deep waters of the fjord. He felt a little sad, because since he had been exiled from his home in Greco, he had only killed once in self-defense, and to eat, and again this time it was survival. He'd had no other choice.

There was a splashing sound behind him, and he turned to see three creatures standing there. He rose up and glared at them; it was a frightening sight.

"Please," said one of the creatures, "we come in peace."

"What do you want?" growled Demodus.

The creature spoke again. "We meant you no harm; we were just curious to see who you were. We have lived here for centuries, and we have never been aware of your existence."

"I have only recently arrived here from off the ice flow," said Demodus. "But if you wish me no harm, why did you try to drown me?"

"We did not know that you could drown; you were in the water the same as we were. We just wanted a closer look at you, and we thought that you wanted the same thing."

Demodus sat down again. What the creature said made sense. "Who are you?" he asked.

"We are the Scaleygill race, and we live in many countries. We came from the sea many thousands of years ago, and adapted ourselves to live on land as well as in the water. We harvest the grasses and seaweed that grow in the fjord, and we eat fish. Our kingdom lies deep in the cliffs, and is entered by a secret entrance that is below the water in the fjord. King Krull, our leader, has invited you to come and meet with him in our kingdom; but you would need to stay under the water long enough to reach the entrance."

"I can swim underwater for five miles before I need to breathe," said Demodus.

"Good," said the Scaleygill. "It is only about a mile. So can I inform the King that you will come?"

"Yes," said Demodus. "I will meet you here tomorrow at sunrise."

"Very well; until then," said the Scaleygill, and disappeared into the fjord.

Chapter 17

KING KRULL

By sunrise the next morning, Demodus had fished and
eaten and was ready to meet King Krull and see his
kingdom. The Scaleygill arrived and asked Demodus
to follow them. They began to dive down into the water
deeper and deeper. They were going directly down, and after
about half a mile, a large cave appeared. They swam into it,
and after fifty yards they came up to a rock face. The Scaleygill
pointed upwards, and they started to ascend. As they reached
the surface, it suddenly became light again. Demodus stood up
and looked around. He was in an enormous cave. It was high
and wide, and faded off into the distance. On the walls were
thousands of tiny lights, glowing with a bluish-white light
that gave a ghost-like look to the Scaleygills. The Scaleygills
had discovered phosphorous stones on the bed of the fjord,
and over the centuries had collected thousands of them and
fixed them to the walls of the cave to give them light. It was a
constant process.

On one side of the cave was a crop of grass piled up high, and next to it was a crop of seaweed. His eyes wandered further into the cave. Scaleygills were everywhere, all busily carrying out various tasks. Several of them stopped to look at him; to them, he was a giant.

"This way," said the Scaleygill who was leading the way, and Demodus began to follow him. They walked for about half an hour before arriving at the Krull cave. It was off the main cave, and considerably smaller.

"Please come in and sit with me," said Krull, and he gestured toward a rock that was shaped like a bench seat. "Have you eaten?" he asked Demodus.

"Yes," came his reply, and he sat down on the rock next to Krull.

"I'm afraid we got off to a bad start yesterday," said Krull, "and I do apologize for what happened."

"No need," said Demodus. "There were so many of you that I panicked and misread the situation. I thought that you meant me harm."

Krull looked at Demodus and said, "Please, let us start again. We wish no harm to anyone. But I must warn you that there are some very serious dangers in and around the fjord."

"For instance, Hawcas is a fearsome creature. He is an Arctic dragon, and he kills for fun. He has large, powerful wings and swoops in at a terrifying speed. His talons are razor-sharp, and he has a beak that can crush a rock. He comes late in the day, when the sun begins to set, and he will attack anything that he can see.

"And then there is Sextalus, a giant squid with six long tentacles, each with a hard, sharp spear on the end. If you should be unfortunate enough to look into her eyes, she can paralyze you long enough to spear you. She comes into the fjord to feed, and will eat anything that she can catch. She always comes alone.

"And then there are the Trizir Brothers, three vicious giant Sabre Tooth Snow Tigers. There were four, but Hawcas killed one of them and flew off with him. So you see that although the fjord is a beautiful place to live in, it also has its dangers, and as a friend, I beg you to be careful."

Demodus thanked Krull for the information, and then with a thoughtful look on his face, said, "What do you know about the Sword of Destiny?"

Krull held his hands out in surprise. "I've never heard of it. Is it something that I should be aware of?"

"Maybe not," said Demodus. "It was just a thought." Then he stood up and said that it was time for him to go. Krull had given him a lot to think about. He held out his hand, and Krull reached out and touched him. "To friendship!" they both said at the same time, and then Demodus was taken back to the secret entrance that led back to the fjord.

★   ★   ★

Demodus sat in his cave. His mind was troubled. Now that he had discovered that he had deadly enemies, he knew that sooner or later he would have to face them in battle. He had to make defense plans, and make the entrance to the cave secure.

He thought about his enemies one by one. First there was Hawcas; he would probably be the most dangerous because he could fly, and would be able to swoop down and surprise him from almost anywhere. The answer came to him in a flash; he would simply copy the Scaleygills. All he had to do was to tunnel down from his cave to below the water level in the fjord, then he could come and go without being seen. He sat there feeling quite pleased with himself.

Second was Sextalus; she would be a different kind of danger. If he looked into her eyes he would be paralyzed, and it would be all over before he could strike a blow. He knew that he couldn't die, but lying injured inside a giant squid wouldn't be a good idea. He would have to lay a trap for her and take her by surprise and kill her. He knew that he would not get a second chance. *The Scaleygills may be able to help me with this one,* he thought.

Third were the Trizir Brothers; the three giant Sabre Tooth Snow Tigers. They were big and fierce; one-on-one he felt that he might have a chance to win, but they hunted together, and that was far too much to handle. Although he felt that he would have to attack them at some stage, before they had the chance to attack him, he would have to work on a different kind of plan for them.

Demodus decided that he would go and visit Krull and ask for his help to rid the fjord of its perils once and for all. He would need every scrap of information on the creatures before he could make his plans to kill them. But first things first, he must secure the cave. He began by flattening the cliff face at the entrance to the cave, then he cut a huge stone disc that he rolled across the opening of the tunnel. It was perfect, and he thought, *that will stop anything from coming into the cave.*

His next task was to dig a tunnel down, well below the water level in the fjord. The first part of the tunnel would have to be cut on an angle down to the level of the surface of the fjord, and that would allow him to walk up and down. The second part would have to go straight down to about fifty yards below water, and then break out into the fjord. Once it was flooded, it would be easy for him to swim back up to the bottom of the slope. So he set to work at the back of the cave, to give himself the best slope possible.

It was late at night by the time he had finished digging, and he was pleased with the result. He was tired and hadn't eaten all day, so he decided to catch a few fish, and then retire for the night. It was the first time that he would use his new secret entrance. He walked down the slope with great satisfaction, and at the bottom he dove down and into the fjord. It was black in the water, but that didn't matter, because he could see in the dark. He had to because he lived a large part of his life under the ground.

He soon caught a large fish and decided that it would be enough until morning. As he turned to go back, a massive, spear-like tentacle flew past him; had he not turned at that precise moment, he would have been impaled. It was Sextalus, looking for food. He dropped the fish and kicked off toward the entrance of his cave. He was desperate to get there before she could make another strike. He was nearly there and was zigzagging frantically; he had no intention of giving her an easy target. Another tentacle went speeding past him, then the secret entrance loomed up in front of him and he shot into it like a bullet. At last he was safe. Had it not been for the new tunnel, he would have been captured, and the next meal for Sextalus. He staggered up the slope toward his cave, and the golden glow of the sword was never more welcoming.

He lay on the floor, totally exhausted, and looked up at the sword. He knew that he had been unbelievably lucky. As he stared up at the sword it seemed to be saying to him, "Use me . . . use me," and then tiredness took over, and he fell fast asleep.

$\star \quad \star \quad \star$

Demodus stirred and grunted. He opened his eyes and sat up, and the memory of last night's encounter with Sextalus in the fjord came flooding back to him. He had been so close to capture, and from now on he had to be extra vigilant.

Chapter 18

THE SWORD SPEAKS

H e stood up and stretched; he was starving, so he decided to catch something to eat and then go and visit Krull. He needed all the information that Krull could give him about his enemies.

Krull greeted him with genuine warmth. "I'm so glad to see you safe and well! I have been so worried about you. My guards reported to me last night of the attack on you by Sextalus and of your disappearance, so I thought that you may have been killed and eaten. I am so relieved that you are still alive and safe."

Demodus looked at Krull; he seemed so small and fragile, yet his friendship meant so much to him. "Thank you," he said, "but I only stand here before you today by a stroke of good fortune. I didn't see her coming, and she took me by complete surprise. Had I not had an escape route, she would have caught me." Demodus told Krull how he had used the Scaleygill idea of a secret entrance to dig one similar to the entrance of his cave. Last night was the very first time he used it, and he had used it to make his escape from Sextalus.

"We need to work together if we are to rid ourselves of these enemies, and so I've come to see you today to ask you for all the information that you can give me about all of them. With your help, I intend to make our home a safe place to live in for good; and by that, I mean kill them all."

Krull began with the Trizir Brothers. "They come here looking for food, and by food I mean Scaleygills; but for the last hundred and seventy years we have been putting a large feast of fish at the same spot, and they always come down the same well-worn trail and eat their fill. Because of this they have been leaving us alone, and as long as it works, we will keep doing it."

"That is very interesting," said Demodus. "If we know the time and place and the path that they take, then we could set up an ambush when they are feeding and have total surprise on our side."

Krull continued, "Sextalus comes as darkness falls. She can see in the dark, and uses this ability to help catch her food. She always comes into the fjord from the same end; that is why we can keep her in sight at all times. She never comes out of the water, so any attack on her would have to be in the fjord. And remember, if you look into her eyes, it will paralyze you."

"And then we have Hawcas; he is the most unpredictable. He swoops in from any direction without warning, and the only thing that we can be sure of is that he comes early in the evening, just before the sun sets."

Demodus stood up and stretched. "I will leave you now," he said, "and thank you, Krull, for the information; it is most interesting. And now I must go and work out a plan. As soon as I have one, perhaps we can meet again at my cave, and I can show you my new secret entrance."

"That would be good," said Krull. "I will look forward to it." Demodus made his exit.

★   ★   ★

For hours he sat in his cave, staring at the Sword of Destiny. The glow that came from it seemed to have a relaxing effect on him. A plan of attack was slowly forming in his head, and a major part of it involved the use of the sword. It was almost as if the sword was guiding him down a path. His thinking was suddenly crystal-clear, and a battle in vivid pictures was playing out in his head. It was acting out the killing of the Trizir Brothers.

He saw himself digging a tunnel underground, directly along the path that the brothers would take to get to the feast of fish that the Scaleygills had prepared for them. Then he saw himself in the tunnel, waiting for the brothers to pass overhead. The Sword of Destiny was in his hands. He was ready to strike. The first two brothers passed over him, and as the third one passed over, he thrust the sword up through the ground and into his belly and through his heart, killing him instantly. He pulled the sword back down into the tunnel without any hesitation, and sprinted down the tunnel until he was in front of the two remaining brothers. He waited until the first brother had passed over and as the second brother came, he thrust the sword upward and into his belly and through his heart, and killed him instantly. The remaining brother had reached the pile of fish, not realizing what had happened to his brothers; and he would never know. Demodus was already underneath him, and the sword was on its way up and into his heart. He never knew what hit him. The brothers were no more.

The picture faded, and Demodus blinked and looked up at the sword. It was time to reach out and take it. As he touched the hilt, it seemed to blend into his awkward, claw-like hands and become part of him. He felt a surge of power that he had never experienced before. He lifted it high into the air and screamed, "Death to the Trizir Brothers!" and there was a bright, golden glow that encompassed both the sword and Demodus. He fell to his knees and said, "I pledge that this will be done."

The next day, Demodus was down in the fjord at the opening to his secret entrance, waiting for Krull to arrive. When he arrived, he was welcomed and shown the way up to the cave. Krull was very impressed with the way that Demodus had dug it out, and he told him so.

They sat talking together in the cave, bathed in the glow of the sword, and Demodus told Krull of his plan to kill the Trizir Brothers. When he had finished, Krull was delighted. "I will help you in any way that I can. I can't imagine how good it will be to not have to worry about them ever again."

Demodus said, "I need to know in advance when they are coming so that I can be waiting there and in a position to strike."

Krull replied, "I know for certain that they will be here in about three weeks' time, so there is plenty of time for you to dig the tunnel and prepare yourself. We will be keeping a lookout for them while we are preparing the feast."

Chapter 19

THE TRIZIR BROTHERS

A t last the day had arrived; the Trizir Brothers had been spotted, and they were heading toward the fjord for their feast. *Not long now,* thought Demodus, as he waited in the tunnel. The Sword of Destiny was molded tightly in his big hands, and he was ready to strike. A Scaleygill was waiting on the path where the Trizir Brothers would pass directly over Demodus, and as soon as they came into sight, he was to bang on the ground, and then run and hide. This would give Demodus a last-minute warning so that he would be ready and listening for their footsteps. The timing had to be perfect. He would have surprise on his side, but that was not enough on its own. His sword would have to find their hearts; wounding them would not be an option.

It was in the next few moments that Demodus realized that the sword in his hands was no ordinary sword. It began to speak to him, and the voice in his head was back. *Concentrate and follow my instructions*, it commanded, *and strike only when I say, "Strike." Now get ready.*

Demodus was coiled like a spring, waiting for the command. He could hear the pounding of the massive paws coming toward him, closer and closer, and then overhead. The first passed over, and then the second. *"Strike!"* The sword shot upwards and was coming back down so fast that Demodus didn't have time to blink. *"Run!"* barked the voice in his head, and he took off at full pace. *"Stop!"* He screeched to a halt. *"Get ready!"* said the voice. *"Strike!"* The sword shot up and down so fast that Demodus had no time to think for himself. *"Run!"* He took off again. *"Stop! Get Ready! Strike!"*

It was all over in minutes. The Trizir Brothers were dead. The plan had been perfect, and the attack had unfolded exactly as predicted in the vision to Demodus.

When he emerged from the tunnel, there were Scaleygills dancing all around the bodies of the Trizir Brothers. After over one hundred and seventy years, they were at last free of them. Krull walked up to Demodus and said, "You must be tired and hungry, and it seems to me that it would be such a shame to waste all this fish." They both laughed out loud and sat down.

"Let the feast begin!" roared Demodus.

After the fish had been eaten, Demodus suggested that the dead brothers' bodies should be buried in the snow and frozen. He thought that they might be useful to them at a later date. "Leave that to me," said Krull. "It will be done." They both sat there for a while, talking about the events of the day and how well everything had worked out. Krull thanked him again, and then they both made their way back home to their caves.

Chapter 20
SEXTALUS

When Demodus got back to his cave, he put the sword up onto its rock. He was feeling tired, and he lay down by the sword and fell asleep in its warm glow. He began to dream that he was fishing for food in the fjord, when suddenly a spear-like tentacle went right through his body. Sextalus had caught him off-guard. A red-hot pain shot through his body, and he was suddenly fighting for his life. He was wriggling like a worm on a hook and slashing at the tentacle with his razor-sharp claws and slowly cutting through it, but Sextalus pulled him up level with her face and he looked into her eyes. They were cold and merciless. He felt his body go stiff and he couldn't move, she was directing him toward her mouth, and then suddenly everything went dark; he screamed and woke up.

He lay there, soaking wet with sweat and breathing heavily. It had all been so real, and he knew that to rid himself of these horrible dreams he must kill Sextalus. Once again he turned to the Sword of Destiny. He sat up and looked at the sword, and then he closed his eyes and said, "Please help me." The sword glowed brighter for a minute, and then a calm feeling came over him. Once again pictures started to form in his mind, and it was as if the sword was telling him what to do.

He saw himself in Krull's cave. They were talking together, and Scaleygills were collecting bundles of grass and weaving them into long and heavy ropes. "We will need six that will reach across the fjord," he was saying to Krull, and Krull nodded back to him in an understanding gesture. They walked toward Krull's cave and left the Scaleygills to their task. "I will need two of the Trizir bodies to make the plan work. We will tie their bodies to the ropes with a gap of three body lengths between them, and then stretch the ropes across the fjord and secure each end, leaving the bodies hanging just below the surface of the water and in the middle of the fjord."

"Their bodies are so large that Sextalus will spot them as soon as she enters the fjord, and being greedy, she will spear both of the bodies at the same time. As soon as both bodies are speared, she will be stretched out wide so that she will not be able to move and strike again; that is, as long as the ropes hold firm."

"They will," Krull assured him. The pictures were flooding into his head. It was getting dark, and he could see himself hiding in the rocks at the entrance to the fjord, watching and waiting, with the sword molded tightly in his hands. As soon as he knew that Sextalus had speared the bodies, he would strike. He crouched, waiting for the signal from the Scaleygills, and suddenly, she was there. Now, would she take the bait? As soon as she was in reach, two tentacles shot out and speared both of the bodies. She tried to pull them toward her, but they wouldn't move; the ropes were holding fast.

Demodus got the signal to move, and dove into the water. He sped through the water in his seal-like way, holding the sword out in front of him. As he reached her, the blade of the sword flashed and sliced through her head like butter, and as she closed her eyes, he brought the blade down across them, shredding them into a thousand pieces. Then he cut off the tentacles from her body, and she sank down into the darkness. He wasn't finished yet; he swam over to the Trizir bodies and cut the ropes, and they sank down into the darkness to join Sextalus in her cold and lonely grave.

Then the pictures disappeared and he was on his own, sitting by the Sword of Destiny. Again he picked it up, and the hilt felt warm as it molded itself into his hands. He felt a surge of power go into his body, and both he and the sword glowed brightly. "Death to Sextalus!" he screamed, and fell to his knees. "This I pledge."

Later that day, Demodus was in Krull's cave, going over his plan to kill Sextalus. Krull was very excited, with three of his worst enemies already dead, and now a chance of ridding himself of Sextalus. It was almost too good to be true. But he was genuinely worried about the safety of his friend. "Are you sure that you want to do this, Demodus?"

"Yes, I'm sure, my friend. How else can we live our lives without forever looking back over our shoulder in fear of our very lives? Now, back to work. Are you sure that you can make the ropes strong enough to hold Sextalus?"

"Yes," said Krull, "but I will need four days, and I will need your help with the two Trizir bodies to get them down to the water. From then on I can manage the rest of it. We will have to do it early in the morning, just in case Hawcas decides to give us a visit. We will have the ropes all ready to tie the bodies onto, and then we must get them into the water and out of sight as soon as possible."

"Very good," said Demodus. "Now I must find a hiding place on the rocks that are behind Sextalus when she spears the two bodies, and also a place where I can see your signal to attack. If all goes well, we will have one less monster to worry about, my friend. Now I must go and rest and prepare myself. Let me know when you need my help with the bodies."

Four days later, Demodus was heaving the massive bodies of the Trizir Brothers over and down the rock face of the fjord to the water's edge. The effort was intense. Hundreds of Scaleygills were in the water, pulling the thick and heavy ropes across the fjord. The first body was tied to the ropes and pushed into the water, then the second followed. It took four hours in all to have the ropes secured on both sides of the fjord with the bodies hanging from them, dead center of the fjord. Krull was very pleased with the day's work, and he turned to Demodus and said, "We need to be in place before sunset. Are you happy with the signal arrangements?"

"Yes," said Demodus. "I will be ready and waiting."

An eerie darkness fell across the fjord like a blanket of death, and the Scaleygill guards stood motionless, watching and waiting for the first indication that Sextalus was on her way.

Demodus was hiding behind a large rock at the entrance of the fjord, with the hilt of the sword molded firmly in his powerful hands. The surge of power that he felt though his body made him feel invincible. All that he was waiting for now was the signal for him to attack; he already knew how the battle would end, because the sword had shown him in his vision.

His full concentration was now on one particular Scaleygill high in the rocks, and on his signal, he would know that Sextalus had been snared, and the attack was on.

The underwater guards had spotted movement; it was Sextalus. They watched as she slid smoothly by. Now it all depended on her and what her reaction would be when she saw the two bodies hanging in the water. She saw them, and precisely as the sword had predicted, two spear-like tentacles shot out in different directions and speared the bodies; she was trapped.

The Scaleygills wasted no time; they flashed a signal to their guard high in the rocks, and in turn he sent his signal to Demodus. He took off like an arrow, diving deep and swimming powerfully like a seal. The Sword of Destiny was glowing, and it seemed to be pulling him to his target.

But there was something different; it was not the same as in the dream. Sextalus had swiveled around and was facing him. She still had four tentacles free, and they were coiled up and ready to strike. Demodus had to make a lightning-fast decision, so he changed direction and dove deep down into the fjord and underneath Sextalus. He knew that he could not attack her from behind in case he accidently cut the ropes that held her. His only choice was to attack her from below, and this meant swimming directly toward her mouth. It was a chilling thought, but the thought was gone in a second, and he was on his way up. Surprise was on his side, and he knew that his first target had to be her eyes. He couldn't take the risk of accidently looking into them. Suddenly, he was there. The sword arched and slashed across her eyes, and they were no more.

But Sextalus wasn't going to go without a fierce fight. A powerful tentacle wrapped around Demodus' legs and it was pulling him toward the point of another one; he had to break free. The sword slashed and severed the tentacle holding him and slashed again, cutting off the spear end of the one speeding toward him.

Demodus wriggled free and swam away. When he turned back, Sextalus was pouring squid ink into the fjord; the water was black. It was her last desperate attempt to stay alive. Demodus dove down deep again and came up behind her, and this time there was no fear of cutting the ropes. Once again the sword seemed to take over; it slashed at Sextalus in a frenzied assault and didn't stop until Sextalus was sinking down to the bottom of the fjord in a thousand pieces. Demodus swam over to the Trizir bodies and cut them loose. He had a big smile on his face and said to himself, *Thank you for your help, brothers.* It was all over; both Sextalus and the Trizir Brothers were down at the bottom of the fjord where the fishes would feed on them, and soon they would be no more.

As Demodus pulled himself out of the water and stood on the bank, the Scaleygills came out in their hundreds, chanting: "Demodus! Demodus!" Krull kept his distance; it was Demodus' moment, and he had no intention of spoiling it for him. After all that he had done for them, he was now a hero in the eyes of his race. But there was, however, a small nagging doubt in Krull's mind.

Demodus was a natural killer; he had proved it. And the Scaleygills were a peace-loving race. He hoped that in the future it would never turn out to be a problem for his friend.

After all the excitement had died down, life in the fjord was good. For many years they all lived in relative safety, and a strong bond was forged between Demodus and the Scaleygills.

However, Hawcas seemed destined to spoil it all. He was making more and more attacks on them. In one bloody week he had killed twenty Scaleygills; it could not go on like this.

Demodus invited Krull to his cave for a meeting to discuss what to do, and how to rid themselves of Hawcas once and for all. As they sat together discussing the problems that they now faced, the Sword of Destiny began to glow brightly.

Demodus had not held the sword since the night he had used it to kill Sextalus. Was it about to tell him something? Krull looked up at Demodus and said, "I think it is time for me to go and leave you alone to talk with the sword." He turned and started to walk down the ramp toward the water, dove in and disappeared.

Demodus sat down and looked up at the sword. "Help me solve our problem," he said, and the glow of the sword bathed him with a warm feeling. Once again, pictures began forming in his head.

He was talking with Krull. "I need you to dig up the remaining Trizir body from out of the ice. I am going to use it as bait to kill Hawcas."

"Very well," said Krull, "but you will have to get it to wherever you want to put it."

"That won't be a problem," said Demodus. He saw himself heaving the body up the face of the cliff to the platform directly in front of his cave entrance. He laid it out carefully to look as if the Trizir brother was sleeping, then he rolled back the stone disc so that there was a gap wide enough to thrust his arm through while holding the sword. The trap was set.

As the sun began to set he waited patiently, ready to spring his trap. It would have to be a lightning strike. Suddenly, a large shadow covered the body; Hawcas was diving. He waited for the body to move; he had to be sure that Hawcas had his claws locked into the flesh before he struck. It moved, and he struck. A loud scream echoed down the length of the fjord, and then he rolled back the stone disc and looked at the body of Hawcas lying down by the water. The pictures faded, and Demodus picked up the sword. Once more a surge of power went through his body. He held the sword high in the air and screamed, "Death to Hawcas! This I pledge."

Chapter 21

HAWCAS

As dawn broke, Demodus was wide awake. He had already eaten, and was preparing to visit Krull. He walked down the slope to the water and dove in, swimming down and out into the fjord. As he was swimming toward the entrance of Krull's cave, several Scaleygills waved to him. He was always a welcome visitor. He reached the entrance and swam up to the cave, and as he lifted himself up onto the bank, a crowd of Scaleygills gave him a noisy welcome. Demodus loved it, and waved to them. He walked on to Krull's cave with purpose in his step. Krull saw him coming, and held out his hands. "I didn't expect to see you so soon," he said, smiling at Demodus.

Demodus held out a hand to his friend and said, "Krull, I have a plan worked out. I am going to kill Hawcas, and I will need your help."

"Anything," said Krull. "What do you want me to do?"

"I want you to dig up the remaining Trizir body from out of the ice, and when you have, I want you to cover it over with sea grass and wait until it is thawed out. I need it to look as though it is still alive, and sleeping. Then when you have it ready for me, I will carry it up onto the ledge, close to the entrance of my cave. And then I will wait for Hawcas to swoop down and attack it, and as soon as he sinks his claws into the body, I will kill him."

"It sounds very dangerous, my friend," said Krull, looking worried. "Hawcas is so big and powerful."

"Trust me," said Demodus. "The Sword of Destiny has shown me the way to conquer him. Now we must prepare, and please make sure that the body is well-covered with grass so that it is hidden from Hawcas."

It took five days before the Trizir body thawed out completely. It had been preserved well in the ice. Demodus looked down at it and thanked Krull; it was the perfect bait for Hawcas. It was still early in the day, but he knew that he would have to work fast if he was to get everything in place before the sun began to set. With the help of the Scaleygills, he set to work. He had decided that the best and quickest way to move the body was to lower it down into the fjord, then float it up level with his cave, and heave it up to the ledge at the entrance.

Three hours later, the body was up there on the ledge. It had been a torturous effort, and the Scaleygills had been a tremendous help. Once again he thanked his good friend Krull. Krull looked concerned and said, "Demodus, please promise me that you will be careful; if you were to be killed, the Scaleygill people will be mourning more than merely a friend."

Demodus looked down at his tiny friend. "Please have no fear; I know for certain that the only danger lies with Hawcas. I can assure you that by nightfall, Hawcas will be dead."

Krull and the Scaleygills started back for their cave. They were all going to be well out of sight by sunset; there was to be no movement or distraction that would stop Hawcas from attacking the Trizir body. Demodus was busily laying out the body to make it look as if he was sleeping, then he moved into the tunnel and rolled the stone disc across the entrance, leaving a gap large enough to be able to thrust the sword through and into Hawcas. When he had finished, he went down the tunnel into his cave; he needed to rest, and there wasn't much time. He lay down by the sword, and its warm glow relaxed him. Soon he was asleep.

Two hours later, he awoke and opened his eyes. There was a voice in his head, and it was saying that the time had come, and Hawcas was on his way. He stood and picked up the sword; its power surged though his body. He felt that nothing could stop him from killing Hawcas now. He held the sword and it molded into his hand; he was ready, and he started up the tunnel toward the entrance. Once there, he positioned himself; there would be only one chance, and he had to get it right.

As predicted in his vision, the body was suddenly cloaked in a shadow. He waited for the body to move, and as it did, he struck. There was a deafening scream of pain, and it was all over. He stood up and rolled the stone back. He looked down, and saw Hawcas lying by the water's edge on his back, dead. But suddenly Hawcas moved; he wasn't dead. Demodus started down the cliff face toward him. *He soon will be,* he thought to himself.

Demodus stood over Hawcas and raised the sword over his head, ready to plunge it deep into the dragon's evil heart. Hawcas was lying helplessly on his back, looking up at Demodus. "Spare me!" he screamed; it took Demodus by complete surprise.

He lowered the sword and said, "Why should I show you any mercy? You have never shown any mercy to the Scaleygills or anyone else, to my knowledge." A voice suddenly sounded in his head; *"Spare him,"* it said. *"Close your eyes and I will show you why."* The sword was speaking to him.

He closed his eyes, and pictures began to form in his head. He saw himself lay the sword across the wound that he had inflicted upon Hawcas, and then watched as it healed. Hawcas stood up and said, "Thank you, my Lord Demodus." Then he saw himself sitting on Hawcas, flying through the fjords. The pictures disappeared, and then the voice spoke again, *"Spare him, and he will become your servant and will obey your every command."*

"Are you all right?" asked a voice. Demodus opened his eyes; it was Krull, and there were Scaleygills all around, taking a closer look at Hawcas. He was huge, even to Demodus.

"I want you to trust me, Krull. I am going to spare Hawcas."

Krull looked at him in disbelief. "Why? Demodus, why? He keeps trying to kill us all, and he would never spare you."

Demodus spoke out loud so that all around could hear him. "From this day on, Hawcas will be my servant, and your protector. It will be my task to make him strong again." He raised the sword, and laid it across the gash in Hawcas' chest. It disappeared; the sword had worked its powerful magic.

Hawcas stood up slowly, still weakened from the sword's awesome power. He looked at Demodus and said, "Thank you for sparing my life. You are my master, and I am yours to command."

Demodus gave his first order: "There will be no more attacks on the Scaleygills, and as of this moment, you will be their protector. Now go and rest, and be back here at dawn tomorrow."

Hawcas bowed his head. "Your wish is my command." He opened his massive wings and kicked off from the ground; his power was breath-taking. He soared high into the sky, and disappeared over the cliffs.

Krull looked at Demodus in total disbelief; could it really be true that his worst enemy was now his protector, and Demodus was his master? The fact seemed to dawn on them both at the same time; they both threw their hands in the air and screamed, "At last we're free from his threat!" The Scaleygills were dancing all over the rocks; they would be celebrating well into the night.

Demodus called Krull over to his side. "Tomorrow when Hawcas returns, I will sit on his back and order him to fly me around the fjords. If everything goes well, I will find out how far he can fly me across the sea.

"You once told me that you had a brother who had taken a large number of Scaleygills to find a safer place to live, and the last time you heard from him was when a seagull brought you a message saying that they were all living safely in a country called England."

"That is correct," said Krull.

"Then if it is possible for Hawcas to fly us there, would you like to visit him?"

"Oh yes," said Krull. "It has always been my dream to see Helek again before I die."

"Very well then," said Demodus. "If it is possible, you will."

Chapter 22

A New Horizon

As dawn broke, Demodus had already been fishing and was eating hungrily; he wanted to get started as soon as Hawcas arrived. The Scaleygills were all over the rocks doing their various tasks, when suddenly a shadow descended over them. They froze in terror; it was Hawcas. But they need not have worried, because he flew past them as though they were not there. He landed on the ledge by the entrance to Demodus' cave, and as soon as he did, the stone disc rolled back and Demodus came striding out. "I want you to fly me around the fjords today. Are you strong enough?"

"Yes," said Hawcas, crouching down so that Demodus could climb up on his back. As soon as he was on, Hawcas kicked off and flapped his wings. Once he was up high enough, he glided gracefully on the air currents that came up from the cliffs.

Demodus was amazed by the beauty of the fjords as he looked down. He could see for miles across the ice flow. Hawcas flew so smoothly; he hardly moved his wings, and yet they were flying at breath-taking speed. It was two hours later when they landed back at the entrance to Demodus' cave. After Demodus had dismounted, he asked Hawcas if he would be able to take Krull and himself to England. Hawcas said, "Yes, I have been there before; it is almost due south, and an easy journey across the sea."

"Then we make the journey tomorrow," said Demodus. "Be here at dawn."

"Yes, master," said Hawcas, and kicked off into the air and disappeared.

When Demodus gave Krull the news, he was delighted. "I never believed it would ever be possible. I am going to meet my brother after all these years! Thank you, Demodus," he said.

Demodus smiled at him and said, "I'm looking forward to our visit, too."

The next day, Krull was waiting with Demodus for Hawcas to arrive, and suddenly there was a large shadow cast over them. Hawcas had arrived. Demodus lifted Krull up onto Hawcas and climbed up after him. "Are you ready?" he asked. "Then let the journey begin."

Hawcas kicked off and soared into the air; there were Scaleygills all over the rocks waving wildly and shouting, "Safe journey!" Soon they were over the sea; it was deep-blue and sparkling in the morning sunshine, and it stretched as far as the eye could see. They flew for about three hours before they saw land again. Little islands were popping up, and then real land; it was the north of Scotland. It was green and lush, with mountains and lakes. It was so different from the fjords, but it was just as beautiful.

Their path took them over villages; some small, others very large. They saw animals in green fields feeding on the grasses, and they passed birds flying all around them. It was getting warmer as they got closer to their destination, and it felt good. Hawcas had started to slow down. They were over a vast forest, and they were going down; below them a large clearing came into view, and Hawcas landed.

Demodus jumped down from Hawcas and stretched out his arms to help Krull off. They stood there for a few moments, looking all around at the lush trees. It was so quiet and peaceful. "Where do we go from here?" Demodus asked Hawcas.

"There is a trail that leads to a large lake. There you will find the Scaleygills. I will stay here until you wish to return."

Demodus crouched down and said to Krull, "Jump up onto my shoulders, little friend; it will be easier to travel this way," and they started off down the trail. They were soon standing by the edge of the lake. Demodus waded in, and they began swimming around. It didn't take long to contact the first Scaleygill, and in no time at all there were hundreds. Krull told them who he was, and they led them to the cave were Helek was. It had an underwater entrance like the one in the fjord, and when they emerged from the water, Helek was standing there, ready to welcome them.

The two brothers held each other in a fierce embrace, neither one wanting to let go. When at last they did, Krull introduced his brother. "This is my brother, Helek, whom I have told you so much about." Then he turned to his brother and said, "This is Demodus, my true and trusted friend, and champion of the Scaleygills."

That night they feasted and danced, and Krull told the stories of Demodus and his sword, and how he had killed the Trizir Brothers and Sextalus and captured Hawcas, and how he had flown here with them on his back. The Scaleygills were all spellbound as he told his stories, and it was late into the night when the party ended.

The following morning, Helek offered to show his guests around his kingdom. Demodus was very interested in the cave; it seemed to have no ending to it. Helek told him that it went on for miles, and that they only used a small part of it. Demodus asked if he could go and explore it while he spent time with his brother, showing him around. "Of course," said Helek, glad to have his brother to himself.

Demodus started off down into the cave and was soon out of sight. It was a catacomb of tunnels and caves, and he covered the ground at a pace. After what must have been ten miles or more, the caves came to an abrupt end. He looked at the rock face, and sensed that something of interest lay on the other side. He crossed his powerful arms above his head and bared his claws, then he leaned against the rock and began to spin. He bored through the rock at great speed until he suddenly broke through into bright daylight. As he looked around, he realized that he was back in the clearing where Hawcas had landed. Hawcas wasn't there; he must have gone looking for food. It didn't matter, because Demodus wanted it to be his secret. He went back into the tunnel and sealed the entrance, then he made his way back to the Scaleygill cave. In the meantime, Helek had been showing Krull his kingdom; it was wonderful. The lake stretched for miles, and high cliffs circled one end. The water was a hundred yards deep, and at the far end it was shallow where they cultivated their grass crop. The water was very warm compared to the fjord, and it felt comfortable. When they got back to the cave, Demodus was already there. Helek asked him if it had been interesting. "Yes," he replied. "It was very interesting."

The time had come to go back home. They said their goodbyes on the bank of the lake, and promised Helek that they would return sometime in the future, and thanked him for his hospitality. As they walked back up the trail, Demodus couldn't help feeling that they were being watched; but nothing untoward happened, and they reached the clearing without incident. Hawcas was there, waiting. "We're ready to go back," said Demodus, and they were soon on their way.

It had been about a month since they had visited Helek, but Demodus could not get it out of his mind. Since they had returned, he had been flying with Hawcas every day, and staying away longer each time. They had visited a large island in the South Seas; in the middle was a smoking volcano, and the entire island was covered in thick jungle. He had felt strangely attracted to it, and decided that he would like to live there for a while. He had to tell Krull, but for some reason, he was finding it very difficult. It couldn't wait any longer; he would tell his friend tomorrow.

At sunrise, Demodus went to see Krull, and told him that he was moving on. Krull looked at him and said, "I have sensed how you have been feeling, my friend, and I have noticed a restlessness within you. But please remember that no matter where you go, you will always be in our hearts, and cherished as our champion. And who knows; one day you may return to us. You must know that there will always be a welcome for you here."

Later that day, Demodus was saying goodbye to Krull and the Scaleygills; he had the Sword of Destiny in a scabbard and belt that he had strapped around his waist that the Scaleygills had made for him out of tiger skin from the last Trizir brother. He was sitting astride Hawcas and looking down at his good friend. "Goodbye, Krull," he said, with sadness in his voice. "May good fortune and happiness forever be your companions." Then, as they climbed into the air, he shouted, "Goodbye, old friend!" and disappeared over the cliffs.

Chapter 23

CLUTE

They landed at the foot of the volcano. It was late in the night, and the island was bathed in the light of a full moon. Demodus looked around him; it was a barren part of the island, rocky and dusty, but he could just make out where the jungle started. He had brought a package of fish with him that Krull had wrapped in long grass and give him for the journey. "We eat now, and then sleep," he said to Hawcas. "Tomorrow we will explore."

The night passed peacefully; they ate the remainder of the fish, and took to the sky. "Look for a clearing, then land," ordered Demodus. They flew around in circles until Hawcas spotted a large clearing and landed. Demodus jumped off and started walking toward the trees; they must have been fifty yards tall.

Suddenly there was a crashing noise coming from inside the jungle, and out of nowhere a massive giant came smashing his way through the trees. His angry roar was deafening. He was coming toward Demodus in long strides and swinging a heavy club. Hawcas was already in the air and preparing to attack. A voice spoke to Demodus, *"Take the sword and strike."* He drew it and pointed it toward the giant; he could feel the power pulsing through his body.

Hawcas struck first. His massive talons ripped into the giant's face. He screamed out in agony and dropped his heavy club and clutched his face; he would never get the chance to pick it up again. Demodus leapt forward. His blade flashed through the air as it severed the giant's leg at the knee. He fell to the ground, writhing in agony, but it soon ended. Demodus jumped up onto the giant's chest and plunged the sword deep into his heart. He was dead, and all fell quiet. Hawcas landed next to his master. "Well done," said Demodus, "but we must be on our guard from now on; there may be others."

Demodus would have liked to go on exploring, but he knew that he needed to build a safe enclosure, and it had to be in the center of the clearing. It would be the perfect place, where he would be able to see in all directions and give him time to deal with any danger that may come from the jungle. But first he must get rid of the giant's body. "Can you lift the body?" he asked Hawcas.

"Yes, master," Hawcas replied.

"Good, then I want you to lift him high in the air and take him out to sea and drop him; the fishes will do the rest." Demodus picked up the giant's leg and laid it across its chest, then he signaled to Hawcas, who hopped onto the body and gripped it with his massive claws. Then with a flap of his wings he took to the sky and disappeared over the sea. When he came back he was minus the giant, and Demodus set about his task with a sense of urgency. He cut down trees from the edge of the jungle with his sword, and Hawcas carried them to the middle of the clearing. In two days they had built a circular barrier ten yards high, and big enough for them both to sleep safely in.

Demodus had been exploring and had found a trail that led to the sea, and he soon found out that there was a plentiful supply of fish to eat. With his swimming and hunting skills, he had caught enough for Hawcas and himself. He knew that he would have to do most of the exploring himself, because Hawcas was far too big to go crashing through the jungle, and should they ever have to do battle, Hawcas was most effective attacking from the air. So Demodus left him behind to guard their camp while he was away.

When Demodus got back, he sensed that something was wrong. Hawcas was in the air, circling above the clearing. As soon as Demodus entered, Hawcas landed back down into the enclosure. "What's wrong?" Demodus asked him.

"We are being watched," Hawcas said, "by a band of red, monkey-like creatures. They walk upright like you do, and they are much taller than ordinary monkeys."

Demodus said, "They sound harmless enough, because if they had wished to hurt us, they would have attacked the enclosure when they saw me leave. Nevertheless, we will not take any chances.

"Now let us eat; I have caught plenty of fish for both of us. And after we have eaten, I will go and try and get them to come out of the jungle so that I can meet and talk with them, and find out what they want. Hawcas, you be ready to take off if you suspect that I am in any danger."

After they finished eating, Demodus stood up and stretched and said, "Come, Hawcas, I think that it is time for me to meet our watchers." He buckled his sword on and strode out of the enclosure. "Where are they, Hawcas?" Hawcas nodded toward the edge of the jungle where he had last seen them, and Demodus started walking slowly across the clearing. He did not want to alarm his watchers and frighten them away.

Chapter 24
QUEEN AZUBA

He was almost there when suddenly the undergrowth parted, and a tall creature emerged and spoke to him. "Greetings. I am Azuba, Queen of the Zodoms."

"And I am Demodus. My friend over there is Hawcas. We both wish you no harm, and we would like to live here on the island as friends."

Demodus looked at Azuba; she was tall and slender, and her face was soft, with a kind smile. Her skin was not like anything that he had ever seen before; it was smooth and brown that shone red in the sunlight. For a moment he was lost for words; his thoughts were all scrambled up. He had never felt this way before.

She spoke again, and his head cleared. "We saw you kill the giant, and you have done us all a great service. He was called Clute; his mother and father live on the other side of the island. For fifty years Clute has terrorized the island; no one was safe, not even his mother and father."

"What made him that way?" Demodus asked Azuba.

"We believe that it began when he was a baby; his father took him up onto the volcano for Kanzil the Lord of the Magma to give him a blessing. But instead of giving him a blessing, Kanzil stole his soul. In exchange, he allowed Clute to grow up much bigger and stronger than his father. But he was to grow up without a soul, and as he grew older he turned evil, and terrorized the whole island. And now you and Hawcas have come to our island and killed him, freeing us from his reign of terror. Kanzil will be very angry with you for killing his slave, and he will not rest until he has killed both of you, so please stay clear of the volcano. That is where he is at his most powerful, and if he traps you, he will steal your soul and make you his slave."

Demodus asked about Clute's father and mother. "Do you think that they will now be my enemies?"

"No," said Azuba. "I have spoken with them and told them of Clute's death. Although they loved their son, they are happy that at last he is no longer a slave to Kanzil. They have expressed their wish to meet with you, and would like you to visit them in their home. They are quite old and friendly, and I think that you would like them. I could take you there, if you would like me to."

Demodus thought for a while, and then he asked, "Do you live in the jungle?"

"Yes, we build our houses high in the trees, away from danger while we sleep. Would you like me to show you?"

Demodus asked her if he could meet her the following morning to go and see her home, and also maybe go and see the giants; she agreed. Demodus went back to tell Hawcas what had happened.

The next day, Demodus was by the forest waiting to see Azuba again, and he was feeling excited as he stood there. She appeared through the undergrowth with two Zodom males carrying spears. She saw Demodus look their way, and she quickly assured him that they were only there for her safety when she was walking in the jungle. "Are you ready, Demodus?"

"Yes," he said, and they started to make their way through the undergrowth. Beautifully colored birds flew between the trees that towered above them, singing as they passed overhead. There were plants of all shapes and sizes and colors, all with their own fragrances. It was warm and damp, and shafts of light pierced the trees like silver spears. As they passed through, he could hear noises of creatures scurrying away from them after being disturbed in the undergrowth, and he felt sure that he could live here forever.

"We're here," said Azuba, as they walked into an enclosure. All the undergrowth between the trees had been cleared, and as he looked up into the trees, Demodus could see all the houses, hundreds of them. Zodoms were crowding all around him, looking him over. He smiled, because it reminded him of the first time he had met the Scaleygills, and they too had done exactly the same. Azuba waved them away, and as they left she said, "As you can see, Demodus, we are a peace-loving race. Now please, follow me." She led him to a massive tree. It was different from the others. The bark around it was deep-blue in color, and all the other trees were pale-green.

"This is the royal tree," she said. "It is over two thousand years old. Do you think that you will be able to climb to the top?"

"Yes," said Demodus, and he stretched out his massive hands and unsheathed his razor-sharp claws. "After you." As they climbed, Demodus noticed how gracefully she moved as she went up in front of him, and with no effort at all. They reached a platform and stood there. She made a strange sound three times, and a trap door opened over their heads. A platform was lowered down to them. They both stood on it and were lifted up. When it stopped, Demodus looked around and was amazed at the size of the house. It wrapped all the way around the massive tree trunk, and stretched out thirty yards into a giant disc that was partitioned off into various rooms, and covered in by an even bigger roof. It was very impressive.

Azuba led him to a table with seats around it. "Please sit down," she said. On the table was a wooden tray piled high with fruit and nuts. "Please eat and drink." He took a long drink from what looked like a coconut shell; it was sweet and cool, and tasted of mixed fruits. He thought how good it was. They ate fruit and talked for about an hour, and then Azuba suggested that they go and visit Clute's mother and father. They climbed down to the forest floor and began their journey. They started off, and travelled for about an hour.

Clute's mother and father lived close to the foot of the volcano. They lived in a house that they had built with stone that had come from the volcano. The roof was timber. They were smaller than Clute, but still giants, and they both towered over them. But they had a gentle way, and looked very old.

"Please come in and sit with us," said Clute's mother. They talked about many things, and asked each other many questions. Then suddenly, without any warning, the ground beneath them shook violently, and they all fell to the ground. There was a great roar, and then everything went quiet and still.

Clute's father looked worried and said to Demodus, "Kanzil knows that you are here. He will be very angry with you for killing Clute."

Demodus stood up and said, "I fear no one," and without hesitation, he strode outside and up toward the volcano, drawing his sword as he went. He stood at the foot of the volcano and roared out loud, "Who are you, Kanzil? Show yourself! I'm not afraid of you *or* your fire!"

Suddenly, a shower of red-hot boulders came crashing down toward him. He stood his ground, and raised his sword up high in front of him. The boulders parted and went crashing down on both sides of him. "Is that the best that you can do?" Demodus screamed. Again another, bigger shower of red-hot boulders came rushing down at him. Once again he raised his sword out high in front of him and the boulders parted and crashed down, passing him on both sides, and then it went quiet.

Chapter 25

KANZIL

A loud voice called out to Demodus, "How dare you stand on my volcano! I am Kanzil, Lord of the Magma and god of Fire. I will crush you and throw you into my fire pit."

"And how will you do that?" Demodus roared back in a mocking voice. Then as he looked up, he could see a large figure standing on the rim of the volcano. It was encased in flames, and it started to walk toward him. He wasn't going to stand there and wait; he started up to meet him. The flaming figure was getting closer when suddenly it stopped dead. Demodus stopped and looked up, and he could see that Kanzil was made of fire.

Kanzil roared, "Who are you?"

"Demodus!" he roared back.

"Where did you steal that sword from? It belongs to me; I forged it myself, and I will spare you your life if you give it back."

"Come and get it!" roared Demodus, "Or go back to your fire pit!"

The ground shook. "You will regret your decision," said Kanzil, and returned to his fire pit. Demodus kept watching him until he was back inside the volcano and out of sight, then he made his way back to the giants' house.

When Azuba saw him coming back, she ran to him and threw her arms around him. "I thought that I would never see you again!" she cried. "But how did you escape from him?"

"Escape!" said Demodus. "It was Kanzil who escaped. He was afraid to fight with me."

The two giants looked at each other. "How could it be? No one defies Kanzil and lives."

After they had said goodbye to the giants, they started the journey back to Azuba's home. As they walked through the jungle, Demodus put his arm around her and held her close to him, and she held him back.

As the days turned into weeks, their friendship for each other turned into love, and one year later, Azuba gave birth to their son. He was part Zodom and part Gnome. His upper body resembled his father, with strong arms and shoulders, and his hands had retractable claws. His face had his mother's features, but his eyes were the same shape as his fathers, and they were bright-red and glowed in the dark. From the waist down he was a Zodom, and he would grow up to be agile like his mother.

They gave him the name Demodom, from Demodus and Zodom, and as the family grew over the generations, they became known as The Demodoms. They all lived happily side by side with the Zodoms. Demodus taught the Demodoms how to tunnel, and they had used their skills to dig fresh-water wells and underground caves for storing food. Azuba taught them how to climb and move through the tree tops, and Hawcas had taken them for trips, flying high in the sky. Life was good for all of them. Hawcas made many journeys back to the north to see his dragon family and friends, and sometimes he stayed with them for years. Demodus told him that he would call him through the power of the sword if he ever needed him urgently, and Hawcas was grateful for the freedom that he gave him.

For the last twenty years, the island had been getting gradually warmer, and there seemed to be a greater amount of fine ash coming from the volcano. It had been very gradual, but it was beginning to affect the plant life. The tops of the trees were beginning to scorch and die, but much worse was the affect it was having on the Zodoms, who spent most of their time in the tree tops. They were becoming sick and dying. On the other hand, the Demodoms spent most of their time either underground or fishing in the sea, so they hardly noticed any difference.

Demodus was getting very worried, and he told Azuba of a land that he had once visited many years ago, called England. There was a vast lake with caves running from it that stretched for miles and led out into a deep forest, with plenty of fruit and berries and nuts to eat. It would be a perfect place for them all to live, and he said that it was only a matter of time before Kanzil's magma ash killed off everything living on the island. Azuba knew that he was right and said to him, "What can we do?"

Demodus said, "Tomorrow I will get Hawcas to take me to England and visit my friends the Scaleygills, to see if everything is the same as the last time I was there. If it is, I will ask Hawcas if he will ask his family and friends to fly me and the Demodoms over to get everything ready, and then I will come and collect you and the Zodoms, and then Kanzil can have his island to himself."

Early the next day, Demodus left the island with Hawcas, on their journey to England. As soon as they landed, Demodus went to see Helek, who was delighted to see him again. He explained the plight that he and his family were in, and how he wanted to bring them over to live in the caves and the forest. Helek welcomed the idea, and said that he and the Scaleygills would help them in any way possible. "Wonderful!" said Demodus. "Then we will waste no time; let us begin."

On the way back home, Demodus asked Hawcas if he could rely on the help of his family and friends to ferry the Demodoms to England, and then later ferry the Zodoms. "Give me two days," said Hawcas, "and I promise you that I will do everything that I possibly can." It was dark when they arrived back, and they ate and slept. Tomorrow was going to be a busy day.

At dawn, Demodus was sitting next to Azuba. He told her of his meeting with Helek, and his offer to help them when they got to England. He told her how fresh and sweet the air was, and how beautiful the forest was. He was sure that they would all be happy and safe there.

Azuba said, "Then let us all leave this island and start again, Demodus. We are all in your hands. But please be quick, because every day that passes, our family is dying."

Demodus called all the Demodoms together and told them of his plan to go to England. "We all go first and make the caves big enough to live in, and then I will go back and collect Queen Azuba and the Zodoms and bring them to England. You will need to use all the mining and tunneling skills that I have taught you. We have very little time, so I expect you all to work as hard and as fast as you can; remember, your mother and the Zodoms are relying on you to look after them." Demodus turned to his son Demodom. "I want you to stay behind and look after your mother. Keep her safe until I return."

"You have my promise," said Demodom.

Two days later, the island was cloaked by a gigantic shadow; there must have been fifty dragons circling over the island. Hawcas had rallied all his family and friends to help Demodus in his hour of need. Demodus put his arms around Hawcas' massive neck and thanked him, then he whispered to him so that no one else could hear, "We have got to move quickly; Kanzil will soon realize that we are planning to do something, and it will not take him long to realize that we all intend to leave the island for good. Will you organize your family and friends to land one by one in the clearing, pick up a load of Demodoms, and take off right away and head for England?"

"Leave it to me," said Hawcas, and he took off into the sky. After two hours, all the Demodoms were on the dragons, with Demodus leading the way on Hawcas.

When they arrived in England, Helek was there to meet them. He had prepared a passageway into his cave so that the Demodoms could get in without having to use the underwater entrance. Demodus thanked him for his help, and told him that he and the Demodoms would be tunneling all the way through to the great forest beyond the hills, and that is where they intended to live. Helek told him of the plan that he had set in motion to feed the Demodoms while they worked. The Scaleygills would bring them fish and water until they had finished their work and could rest and feed themselves, and hopefully this would speed up their progress. Demodus thanked him again, and went off to organize the digging.

A day after Demodus left for England, Kanzil realized what was about to happen. He knew that the sword had left the island with Demodus, and that without its protection, the island was defenseless. He began to increase the activity in the volcano, and released thousands of tons of hot ash into the air. The tree tops began to burn; a yellow gas was descending onto the jungle floor, and the Zodoms and animals were choking to death. Demodom started leading his mother and the Zodoms deep down into the underground caves that he and the Demodoms had mined out over the years. Down in the caves there was plenty of food and water for all of them, so they would be safe until Demodus came back for them.

Kanzil rained hell down onto the island. The jungle was burning out of control, and all of the Zodoms' homes were being burned down to the ground. Kanzil was relentless in his destruction of all that lived on the island. In seven days and nights he had poured out enough red-hot ash to completely cover even the tallest of trees that were still standing. The island was a wasteland, smoldering and dead.

Underground all was calm; they could not even begin to imagine what had happened up on the surface. But Demodom was concerned about the amount of air that was left for them to breathe. He had tried to tunnel up to the surface, only to be beaten back by the intense heat, and he was unable to tunnel out to sea because flooding the caves would drown them all. He would have to wait until Demodus returned; there was no other choice.

★   ★   ★

The mining was going on at a relentless pace, and Demodus was leading by example. They tore the rock away as if it was soft clay, and two weeks later it was ready. "Now you can rest!" roared Demodus. The Scaleygills had played their part, feeding the workers as they toiled almost non-stop. Demodus said, "Helek, you are a true friend. I will always be there for you if you need a friend to help you. But I must go now; there is no time to lose." He called out for Hawcas, and climbed up onto his back. "Let's go and get the rest of my family!" he cried, and Hawcas kicked off into the night sky. Demodus was desperately tired, but all he could think about was Azuba and his son, Demodom. At last they would be safe, and free from Kanzil.

Chapter 26

HEARTBREAK

It was shortly after dawn when they arrived back at the island. They looked down in disbelief; the only visible thing was the volcano. "Take me down!" said Demodus. Hawcas landed at the foot of the volcano, and Demodus jumped off. He looked over to where there had been a lush jungle, and there was nothing, only a desolate, smoldering plain of ash. Then suddenly there was a loud, mocking laugh. Demodus turned and saw the fiery figure of Kanzil. "What have you done?" he screamed.

Kanzil snarled back at him, "Did you really think that you could beat me? Now you have nothing." Demodus felt his rage reach fever pitch as he realized that he had lost his family to this cowardly monster.

He drew his sword and felt the power rise in him. "I'll kill you, you coward! You waited until I was away and they were all defenseless!" He started to run toward the volcano, and Kanzil turned and fled back into the fire of the volcano.

Hawcas screamed, "Demodus!" Demodus jumped up onto his back. *"Stop!"* shouted a voice in his head. It was the sword. Demodus froze. "Speak to me," he said.

The voice said, *"Azuba is alive, and so is Demodom. They are in the caves below. Take the sword and point it to the ground."* He drew the sword and pointed it at the ground. A hole appeared that went down to the forest floor, and he could see where the entrance to the caves was. *"Quickly,"* said the voice, *"you have very little time."* Demodus slid down the wall of ash, his claws digging into it to break his fall. He landed safely and started to bore into the ash that was blocking the entrance, and he was through it in seconds. He ran down into the cave, and what he saw made him scream. The Zodoms were lying in a circle; they were all dead. They had been suffocated, choked by the terrible sulphur fumes that had seeped into the caves. In the middle of the circle was his beloved Azuba, cradled in the arms of his son, Demodom.

He leapt over the dead Zodoms, but he was too late. Azuba was looking up at him. Her eyes had lost the sparkle that they once had. Then her lips moved, and in a tiny whisper she said, "Demodus, my love, you have come for us." Her breath drained away in a sigh, and she was dead. Then Demodom opened his eyes and looked up at his father. "I tried so hard, Father, but I have failed you." His eyes rolled back and his head slumped back and he too, was gone.

"No!" screamed Demodus, clutching Azuba and his son in his arms. Cold rage rose in him like never before. He laid the bodies gently down on the ground and stood up. "You will pay for this, Kanzil!" He looked down at Azuba and his son and said a last goodbye, and then turned and left the cave.

He started up the wall of ash, and with every step he took, his rage rose to new heights. As he reached the surface, he knew what he had to do. He climbed onto Hawcas and told him to fly around the volcano, close to the rock face. As he skimmed the rocks, he thrust his sword into the volcano. A hail of red-hot rocks rained down on them, but the sword had created a shield around them. As they circled, the top half of the volcano slowly caved inwards and blocked it off completely.

"Take me up!" he shouted, and they zoomed up into the sky. All the other dragons followed them, and when they were well out of distance, Demodus said, "Stop!" They were circling around, all looking toward the island, when suddenly there was a deafening roar, and the whole island erupted. Smoke and ash shot upwards for miles into the sky, and turned it black. The whole island had completely disappeared into the sea, and everything with it. Demodus lifted his sword high in the air and shouted, "Now, Kanzil, *you* have nothing." He turned to Hawcas and said, "Thank your family and friends for helping me, will you? Then fly me home to England."

Demodus couldn't remember the last time he cried, but he wept all the way back to England. He had lost both the love of his life and his son, all in one evil moment in time.

When he arrived back in England he was silent, and entered into a period of dark depression. He turned on the Demodoms and treated them like slaves; every time he looked at them, he could see Azuba and Demodom.

Chapter 27

AN END TO THE MADNESS

He awoke with a start. His head was spinning, and there was pain in his heart. Because of his dream, he realized what a fool he had been. The Demodoms were his own flesh and blood, and were a wonderful gift from his beloved Azuba. Things would have to change.

He sat quietly in his chair and relaxed, but his head was still confused. Then a voice spoke to him; it was the sword. *"Did you enjoy the journey that I have just taken you on?"*

"So it was *you* who made me remember the past. Why did you not do it earlier?"

"You needed time to mourn," said the sword, *"and now it is time for you to remember who the real enemy is, and remember who banished you from your home and made you take that long and lonely journey.*

"With the power that we possess together, the kingdom of Greco and the king's throne could and should be yours. Why do you think that you are building an army, and who do you think has been guiding you? All the things that are taking place down in the caves you have

been doing under my guidance; now it's time for you to take over and get your army together and take Greco, by force if necessary.

"There is one more thing for you to know. Furnusabal has been sent here by Kanzil. I don't know how he found out where you were, but Furnusabal's fire pit leads directly to the center of the earth, and Kanzil. Furnusabal is the son of Jesabal, and she was Kanzil's daughter. *"The fairy army trapped Jesabal in her volcano kingdom and killed her; this was at the end of the humans' Great World War, and Kanzil will never forgive them. And so he sent Furnusabal to pretend to make friends with you, and then to get you involved against the fairy world. He knows that you hate them because of what the Golden Fairy did to you. And then when Peggy Goody just by chance happened to get involved with the fairies, he took advantage of the situation and made her your enemy to further distract you from what he is really trying to do to you.*

"Kanzil intends to somehow separate you from me and steal me back; if it means killing you, he wouldn't care. And then he can take me and throw me down into the fire pit, where Kanzil will melt me and I will disappear back into the molten center of the world. On that day then he will have all of his power back. That is why I made you put up all the surveillance equipment around the fire pit to monitor his every move; we must stay vigilant! We will need to concentrate on a plan to overthrow Greco city and crown you king, and when we do, Greco will become our power base.

"There is one more thing that you need to know; you have a rogue training officer working with the Demodoms on the firing range. I do not know how, but Furnusabal has managed to penetrate the caves and gain access to the soldiers. But we must remember that Kanzil has enormous power. Between them they have got into his head and are controlling him.

"*He intends to send three trained Demodoms to the home of Savajic Menglor with orders to kill Peggy Goody, who will be staying there as his guest.*

"*They will make their attempt but fail, because Peggy Goody will kill all three of them. We will let him manage to get their bodies back to the caves and dispose of them before he thinks that you could find out.*"

"That is worrying," said Demodus. "But even more worrying is that Furnusabal knows what is going on in the caves."

"*But best of all,*" said the sword, "*he doesn't know that we are on to him, and that gives us an advantage.*"

"His aim obviously is to pit the wizard world against me, as yet another distraction."

The sword spoke again, "*Demodus, you have to decide how big an army you need, and as soon as you reach your target, you must return all the humans back to their own world with the gold that you have promised them. I will wipe all their memories of the caves and what they have been doing. They will simply all awaken in their beds safe and sound, and very much richer.*"

"We can achieve this in the next ten months," said Demodus, "and then my army will be ready to march on Greco."

The following day, Demodus called all of the Demodoms together, and he sat them down and began to tell them how the deaths of Queen Azuba and his first son Demodom had made him mad in the head, and how it had made him behave so badly toward them. "I want to explain to you all that every time I looked at you, I would think of Queen Azuba, and that made me resent you. But I realize how wrong I have been, and that by loving you it should remind me of her, and the love that she had for all of us. This is what she would have wanted for us. Please, my children, forgive me.

"Over the years we have become fewer in number, and because of this we have become more precious to each other. I have foolishly put our family in peril, and that has cost us the loss of many precious lives. I promise that from today onwards things will change. We will become a family again, and all barriers between us will cease to exist. We will visit the Scaleygills and go swimming with them again. There will be no more attacks on the humans. Peggy Goody will no longer be an enemy of ours. I feel that I have tried to harm her unjustly. We will leave the fairy world to get on with their business. Together we have much to do, and I have many things to show you.

"With the help of my sword I will handle Furnusabal." *In my own way,* he thought. A new era had begun for the Demodoms; now only time would tell how destiny would play out when Demodus and his clone army were ready to march on Greco.

The End